I0709599

THE LIGHT OF MIERA:

A Guard's Refrain

BOOK ONE

Written By Ash Hester

Edited By Amy Wilson

Cover Art By ArtWomble

Published By Treat Your Geek

Print ISBN: 978-1-7385534-0-2

Ebook ISBN: 978-1-7385534-1-9

A Guard's Refrain

Copyright © Ash Hester 2024

1st Edition

Content Warnings:
While the utmost care has been taken when dealing with darker storylines, we appreciate some readers would prefer to be warned of triggering content and adult themes. Those already present in the whole series include MC death, magical manipulation, drug misuse, child endangerment, reference to miscarriage and stillbirth, mild graphical description of gore, reference to SA/R, MH themes including anxiety, depression and addiction.

In loving memory of Nelly:
"Freedom's just another word for nothing left to lose."
- Janis Joplin

A Guard's Refrain

INTRODUCTION

Dear Reader,

Prepare to go on a journey. An epic journey... An epic journey much less cliché than this intro.

I've been privileged to see this world, this story, take shape. The concept has grown from some brief raunchy romp of a light novel to a sharply written, layered fantasy epic across several books. Side characters have grown from nameless NPCs to fleshed-out 3-dimensional people. Whole, living cities have grown out of what were single stop-offs on the quest map with creative placeholder names such as "xxxxx". The core romance to the story has blossomed in depth and realism although the ever-increasingly devious machinations of the author continue to work against them.

I can't say I've known many authors, or been this close to their writing process. But I've seen TLOM grow alongside its author from a rough concept and a dream, to draft passages on fanfiction sites and onto weekly read-alongs on Twitch around which a community began to grow and I witnessed the birth of a fandom, with debates over "Best Girl" and collective fawning over the "Dommy

Mommy".

And finally, to this completed novel you now hold in your hands. It's been an incredible journey but now it's finally real. I could make some cheesy reference to the author going on their own "hero's journey", which is perhaps not too far from the truth, but not something I feel I can do justice.

Reading this book now I see all the care, dedication and, at times, sheer will that went into it. The hours of learning and research have paid off.

Buckle up reader, you'll want to give this one at least a second read-through.

Mulukh

THE LIGHT OF MIERA

A Guard's Refrain

BOOK 1

TESTIMONY

Year 3674

* * *

I stand before you today, guilty.
It was my duty to watch over the children of Alamantra.
And, for millennia, I did just that. I watched as kingdoms
flourished and armies rose. I watched as famine spread and
lives were lost. I saw generations pass and species perish.
Until, one day, I could watch no longer.
I interfered with the lives of mortals,
I betrayed my sacred oaths.
Was I right to do so?
Should I be condemned?
I suppose that's for you to decide…

* * *

PROLOGUE

Twilight.

The moon peered over a cloudy sky, casting patchy shadows. Four hooded figures silently snaked their way through a maze of dry flowerbeds to the centre of the dark gardens. Each wore long cloaks in dark colours, as is tradition for such clandestine encounters, as the wind stilled and animals fell quiet around them.

The four figures convened in a secluded gazebo: perfect for their secret meeting.

As an outsider looking in, would you have missed the four figures cloaked in sinister shadows? Perhaps you would have noticed but paid them no mind. Maybe you'd rather not get involved? Nor would I blame you.

If you had noticed, would you have noted one figure wore a finer, more elegant garb than the rest? That they held their head high as the others fawned over them? Perhaps, like me, curiosity would get the better of you and you would narrow your scope to decipher their hushed tones. No mortal ears could hear them as they held up their glowing hands, chanting as they cast their wards between the wooden posts.

"Sisters, what news have you?" asked the one in the

elegant garb, the silken fabric wrapped around her black as shadows.

"We've secured three of the shrine locations. However, the spirits inside remain inactive," replied one dressed in a plain cloak - hers being a greyish colour.

"Freya is proving problematic. However, I believe we've found the shrine of Pudron, and I have sent scouts to try the entrance," added a second, softer voice in a navy cloak.

"The spirits haven't woken for us before," scolded the first. "Why should Igniros be any different?"

"Perhaps we'll have more luck with Auldafrey," offered the soft-spoken one.

"You're kidding yourself; the spirits have no reason to show themselves. We're going to have to do this by force!" the third burst out, her tone eager. "Let's blast the entrance with all we've got!"

There was a rumble of disagreement from the first two as they jumped to refute her suggestion.

"You may have something there…" agreed the elegant one. Although she kept her voice low, it was strong, seductive, and full of intent, the weight of her words causing the three underlings to turn.

"I do?"

"She does?"

The brazen one was almost as shocked by the realisation as her comrades. The three held their collective breaths, eagerly awaiting their marching orders.

"You're right, they have no reason to show themselves. They have been sleeping far too long," she hissed, malice growing in her whispered tones.

"Perhaps it's time we give them a reason..."

* * *

Knowing how it would all end, if I could go back,
would I stop this meeting? No.
This quiet encounter was but a catalyst,
a single step on my path to disgrace,
and my downfall nonetheless.

* * *

That same night, in the Kingdom of Sudra, King Drazah whiled away his day stressing over the labours of ruling, praying his luck would change.

Sudra was a desert land with hot summers, scorched sands, and starving citizens. With their slate-coloured skin, forked tails, and short, pointed horns rising above their temples, you'd be forgiven for thinking the Sudra looked like demons - but this was considered their lesser form. Legends of their power warned others away - leaving their kingdom at peace - however, the whole kingdom had a secret. A secret each Sudra knew, yet none would repeat, or even whisper: they were losing their powers.

It was dark out when Queen Nymati entered their bedroom to find Drazah sleeping at his desk. He still held a quill in his hand, his head tilted back, leaving his mouth ajar as he slumped against the chair. The satin sheen of her nightdress draped behind her as she crossed to meet him. She ran her hands under Drazah's cream, cotton smock and on to his muscular chest. He slowly came around, opening azure eyes to admire his queen.

Nymati cocked her head, her ebony lips parting into a smile. The ruby of her eyes sparkled as bright as the many golden hoops and bracelets she was adorned with, each glowing against her dark skin with radiant charm. She held herself with confidence - not arrogance for it was justified – her straight raven hair slipping over her shoulders as she bent to meet him.

There were myriad stories told across Alamantra of Queen Nymati, Emissary of the Desert. She was known throughout the lands for the kindness of her bountiful heart, and the mercilessness of her calculating mind. She was named - quite justly - the Demon Queen of Sudra.

Nymati was a temple; enduring, stoic, and strong. A temple whose beautiful facade disguised an unforgiving labyrinth within, one wrought with twisted corridors only the bravest of warriors dared enter.

"You work too hard, my king," she cooed.

Her voice was like honey being whispered into his ear. A soft glow came over her hands as she activated her artes, holding him close.

Over the years, Nymati had found some incredibly inventive ways to use her artes, but de-stressing her paramour was perhaps the most important thing she had used them for since becoming queen. Recent years had not been good to their kingdom. Famine was an imminent threat, but she found purpose in doing her duty and helping Drazah any way she could. After all, they were her people too.

"The burden of wearing a crown is far greater than the weight it holds, my queen." Drazah turned to her lovingly, but he still wrinkled his brow.

"Then it's fortuitous we're going to have to trade yours for crops if this drought continues." Nymati lifted the crown from his head.

"Let's hope it doesn't come to that." The king gave a hearty chuckle, pulling Nymati down to sit on his knee. He wrapped her into a tight embrace.

"Don't worry, I'm sure something will come up," she assured him with a kiss, her dainty hands warm against his cheek. "Come, let's get you to bed."

Nymati took his hand in hers, leading him across the room. With each step, her artes swept up his arm, swirling over his chest as he sank to the foot of the four-poster bed. Nymati shuffled over the mattress to kneel behind him. The soft glow of her artes heated his skin as she massaged his broad shoulders, relaxing his muscles.

The Sudran King loved his queen from the moment they first met. Drazah attributed everything he was, and everything he could ever be, to her. She was all he could wish for and more. He often wondered if even love was enough to quantify all that he felt for the goddess that was she.

Nymati ran her hands into his umber hair, working

her way over his skull and around his horns. Her nimble fingers combed back down to his neck and along his spine, her artes ever-flowing into him – it was intoxicating.

"You really are tense, my king."

"I just don't know what to do." Drazah released a mighty sigh. Rubbing his temple with his fingers, he sank forward to rest his elbow on his knee. "Either we fight a war we cannot win, or we surrender to the Duran Empire. No matter what I do, our kingdom, our secret is at risk."

"There's always a third option," Nymati corrected, coming around to straddle his knee.

Nymati pushed Drazah back to lie on the bed, a single fang glinting in the light. She drew in close, his heart pounding against her fingertips as she placed her hands on his chest, leaning in.

A shiver held Drazah to attention. There was no high like it. Just the thought of it made his pulse thump - a resounding baseline to the symphony rising within him. A fanfare beat within his stomach as Nymati drew closer, opening her mouth before his.

"Our secret may be our greatest weakness, but it is also our greatest strength," she whispered, his lip quivering in response, the anticipation too much to bear.

Then Nymati inhaled. Energy rushed to leave his body in an explosion of endorphins. His senses rumbled into a roaring crescendo. His whole body burned, alive and alert.

A moment of pure euphoria held in perfect equilibrium.

Drazah couldn't help but smile. Of course his queen knew what to do.

Their secret had indeed kept them safe all this time, but over the last year, Dura had expanded its reach over its northern borders and it was fast gaining strength. It was only a matter of time before the Empire turned their attention west and came for them, and Sudra was in no position to be fighting anyone, least of all the Empire.

Drazah was released and everything slowed, the world vanishing around them as he saw only her. He imagined this was how the great rocks of the desert perceived the shifting dunes - held in time as the world around them drummed on.

Still perched over him, Nymati kissed Drazah's lips, before working down his neck and along his chest. Drazah sank deeper into the bed, his body gaining weight with every touch. His vision fuzzy, his chest heaved and his skin glowed, as she made her way down toward his navel.

"You are the greatest king Sudra has ever seen. You are strong. You are brave. There's *no* way this Duran fool could ever compete with you," she purred, looking up at him, her fingers curling over the top of his trousers.

Her lips stretched into a sinister smile. "Perhaps what the emperor doesn't know really will kill him."

Her words sent shivers down his spine, resonating deep within as his senses slowly returned to normal. Drazah welcomed the embrace of Nymati's ebony lips, relaxing as a surge of euphoria rushed through him. He allowed it to engulf him, body and soul, as he lost himself to the waving pattern of the painted ceiling. His body warm and clammy, his head light and sweaty, his toes curled.

She was right.

He *was* strong.

He *was* brave.

More importantly, *he knew what he had to do.*

* * *

BEGINNING OF THE END

14 MONTHS BMF

* * *

Alamantra's future lay on a knife-edge.
For six months I waited,
praying the Gods would intervene.
But they never came.
And so, I turned my sights to the Kingdom of Freya,
where all hope for the future
gathered in the bedroom of Princess Arafrey.

* * *

CHAPTER ONE

There were few mortals under my watch that I followed as often as the Frey, Reyla Fenwilt.

Presently on duty, Reyla wore the military garb of the Freya Palace Guard, a simple attire made of leaf-leather and a chest plate of arte-formed wood. She maintained a quiet demeanour and drew little attention, her armour hiding any hint of a feminine shape she may have had. Quietly stationed by the door to the princess' bedroom, her sharp features skulked behind a mane of wild, chestnut hair as she surveyed her charge.

High Priestess Elsafrey sat across from her daughter, a tension pinched about the bridge of her nose. She and the princess were enjoying evening tea - or at least pretending to - as they did several times a week. A platter of fresh fruits and desserts lay ignored between ceramic teapots and saucers as tensions grew.

"Your father is getting impatient," warned Elsafrey, her gaze narrowing over the table between them.

With rolling emerald eyes, Princess Arafrey circled a spoon around the lip of her teacup, a sure sign she had stopped listening to her mother a while ago, but was feigning interest to keep the peace. The two were close, but

Arafrey had long suspected that her mother kept their appointment to keep track of her studies and social life, the latter of which had Elsafrey rather concerned.

"You cannot attend the Summer's Night Festival alone again this year," Elsafrey continued, her voice soft and musical, but ripe with all too familiar disapproving undertones.

Arafrey didn't respond but her eyes flicked over to the door, levelling with Reyla's.

Reyla started and averted her gaze, with a silent promise not to bring this up at a later date. She shifted her weight, instead catching the eye of Mika, the northern Frey with long seaweed coloured hair, stationed beside her.

Like Reyla, Mika wore the uniform of wood and leaf-leather, except he boasted the red cape of the Queen's Guard and Reyla the green of the Princess' Guard, their uniforms featuring similar red and green motifs. They each held the standard issue shield with a metal frame and white dove in the centre, and each held their swords strapped to their sides in leaf-leather sheaths.

"I find it hard to believe no one has asked you yet." Elsafrey's disapproval remained as paramount as she was oblivious. "What about Bodair?"

High Priestess Elsafrey was perhaps the most beautiful of all the Frey. She had green skin so pale it was almost white, and eyes as deep and green as the forests they lived in. Her hair flowed like waves of green moss as she collected her teacup, the vibrant lengths held in place by a silver crown adorned with crystal-clear diamonds.

The crown had been a gift from the Rugla many hundreds of years ago. When Elsafrey eventually retired, the crown would be passed on to Arafrey, who would take her place as Queen and High Priestess of Freya. Although Arafrey feared she may never be ready for such responsibilities.

Arafrey resembled her mother, with familiar soft features and wavy hair, but she lacked the effortless grace and refinement of Elsafrey. She had the potential to be an excellent queen, but she resented the role she had been given and was prone to resistance. To say she was a bad princess would be wildly inaccurate, however, she would often be seen sporting a placid look of indifference, or even quiet contempt, whilst fulfilling her duties.

As if reading Reyla's mind, Arafrey tucked hair behind her pointed ears. Rows of silver piercings caught in the light, highlighting Arafrey's most recent act of rebellion.

Elsafrey sighed deeply in response. Pushing her plate away, she decided to forgo her usual lecture, no doubt fearing her words were already falling on unwilling ears. Instead, she rose to her feet, replacing her chair under the table.

"Very well, suit yourself." The two guards sprung to attention as Elsafrey turned her way. "Reyla, I sent Ceal home early. Would you mind helping the princess change for bed?"

"Of course not, M'lady." It wasn't uncommon for this to happen. As the princess' aide in the past, Reyla often helped where she could, although she couldn't deny holding ulterior motives.

Reyla placed her shield on the wooden dresser. The queen passed on her way towards the door and paused, admiring Reyla as Mika held the door open.

"You really are invaluable, Reyla. Maybe you should come work on the Queen's Guard with me." Elsafrey winked, turning back to look at her still sulking daughter. She beamed as if to spite Arafrey's mood.

"Good night, dear," Elsafrey continued, talking to herself as she glided past. She paused, adding to Reyla, "Make sure she eats something substantial before bed."

Reyla gave a quick salute, nodding as the high priestess proceeded down the hall. She closed the door behind her and dropped the latch. As Reyla returned to the room, the princess had already left her food and crossed to meet her.

"You know, I think she likes you," Arafrey cooed, her arms behind her back as she slinked closer.

"Maybe so, but it makes me feel really bad being praised by her," Reyla admitted. "Especially knowing I was about to do this..." Reyla held Arafrey's face, gently greeting her green lips with the kiss she'd been anticipating since her shift began.

"You do seem stressed by the whole situation," Arafrey teased, kissing Reyla back.

Reyla wrapped her arms around the princess and smiled, just as she always did.

Reyla ran her hands along the princess' delicate waist, her green limbs weaving around the other like ivy. Her fingers found their way to the nape of Arafrey's neck instinctively, sliding down to unbutton her dress. The buttons and ribbon were undone expertly, and the dress was tossed aside.

In Reyla's eyes, their relationship was one of the worst things she had ever done and the guilt of hiding it was ever-present. The Frey held strong opinions on the matter. Beliefs that, until recently, she shared herself. Even as her hands swept over the soft peaks of her princess, Reyla feared herself evil, an affront to the cycle of life to which the Frey devoted themselves to. She had tried to walk away on many occasions but never found the strength to see it through. She took solace in the fact that someday soon Arafrey would get married, and the decision would be made for her.

Reyla pulled Arafrey in closer, lifting her into her arms, leaning back against the wall as they fell further into each other. Their lips forever locked. Hands flit one over the other. The silk of Arafrey's white undergarment rose as she wrapped her arms around Reyla. Their hearts beating as one, Reyla's lips traced Arafrey's neck, breathing her in as she swept along her collar.

Arafrey was just undoing the ties on Reyla's chest-plate when there came a loud knock on the door.

They paused, chests heaving.

The knock came again, this time followed by a man's voice. "Excuse me, ma'am. Shift change for Reyla."

Reyla pinched her face in the direction of the door. "Gimme a second. The queen sent Ceal home early again."

They remained still in their passionate embrace against, hoping Nasir had not noticed anything.

"What's tomorrow?" Reyla whispered.

"Tea with the twins."

She rolled her eyes. "Yeah, that'll do it."

Reyla let Arafrey down gently, placing a kiss on her forehead.

"I guess I'll see you in the morning," she said, flashing her trademark reassuring smile before collecting her gear and leaving.

Arafrey closed the door, but not before hearing, "*Cheers, mate*" as Reyla stormed down the corridor.

She returned to face her now empty room, throwing herself on to the bed. With a deep sigh, she reached out and grabbed the soft bed sheets, pulling them up and into her chest, as if wrapping them around her would bring Reyla back. Arafrey held them tight as she tried to hold on to the feeling of Reyla's lips on her skin, retracing the light brush of Reyla's fingers against her cheek.

Their time together was limited and every second left Arafrey's head floating and her knees weak - but her father would never allow their relationship. The task of carrying on the Frey line fell to her, and the pressures she faced to choose a husband and procreate were taxing. She knew she would have to reproduce eventually but the idea had never appealed to her - in fact, the thought repulsed her. Not that what she thought ever mattered.

As a princess, Arafrey had few freedoms. She was told how to dress; the dresses often bought for her. She was taught the proper way to walk and talk; often lectured on the way she had to behave.

But with Reyla she could be herself.

'Until it's time to grow up,' she thought, reminding herself of the promise she and Reyla made long ago. Although Arafrey always hoped that day would never come.

Arafrey released an unhappy groan as she rolled over to bury her head in the fluffy pillows.

'If only I wasn't a princess,' she pleaded.

'Things would be so much easier…'

* * *

With a sombre sigh, High Priestess Elsafrey regarded the orange skies from the palace balcony.

Dusk was drawing in, yet the whole forest glimmered with the soft mystic-blue hue of the Life Tree above, giving her a splendid view of the palace gardens. Her eyeline traced the stone path through the lilies, along to the pond where fireflies bobbed along the surface. The grounds were quiet except for the ambient hum of chiming crickets and the many birds still singing as they made their way to their nests.

"Ah, Elsa. I thought I'd find you here," said King Galafrey, a strong monotone voice announcing his arrival. "Long day?"

"The longest."

King Galafrey's sagely robes enveloped Elsafrey as he drew her into a loving embrace. She responded in kind, still watching the fireflies.

"And how is our daughter?" he asked, linking their fingers.

The Frey king was a regal man of few words. Standing a few inches taller than the average Frey, his skin was more of a pistachio green than the others and his eyes were a deep mahogany. He always wore his hair down, the straight oaken lengths framing his face held in place by the golden halo of his crown.

"As obstinate as always."

"I keep telling you we should reassign that guard of hers. Why must you always indulge her?"

"Because she is our daughter," Elsafrey insisted. "She will find her way."

Galafrey avoided response by kissing her hair, a sure sign he disagreed, and Elsafrey chose not to push the matter any further.

As Frey, the two leaders were polar opposites. Elsafrey was kind and gentle. Galafrey was strong and brash. But as husband and wife, king and queen, they were in perfect sync.

The pair had been forced into each other's company as children, despite having little in common. Elsa, as her name was back then, was the daughter of a nobleman who made quite the name for himself selling tonics. Their fathers decided they would be a good fit and Elsa was taught the ways of healing and Frey teachings - practically groomed for the role of high priestess.

"When I hold you like this, I almost forget there are such horrors in the world," Galafrey said, his voice burdened in a way only Elsafrey could hear. "Word of The Duran Empire being formed after Gabris invaded Estra and Puwhar has been confirmed."

"They may as well be a world away with Sudra between us," Elsafrey assured him, squeezing their fingers together.

"The Sudra are a force to be reckoned with, certainly, but they've been at peace for too long, and their people suffer at the hands of the desert," Galafrey returned. "Rumours of an alliance between the Empire and Agrana have already begun to spread. It's only a matter of time before the emperor turns his sights west."

"But Sudran men are formidable. Surely they could take on the Duran Empire?" Elsafrey turned to face her king, looking to him for certainty.

"They could take Duran soldiers ten to one. But with Agrana technology at their disposal, it's anyone's guess what the Empire could do."

Elsafrey rested her head on his shoulder, nestling her nose into his neck.

He pulled her in closer and together they released a joint sigh of concern.

"These are indeed troubled times, my love," said the king looking to the sky, his mahogany eyes catching in the light of the Life Tree. "Troubled times indeed…"

* * *

CHAPTER TWO

Today Drazah would make history.

He drew a deep breath, the warm breeze smelling only of the elephant he sat upon. Behind him, the drumming of one thousand Sudran soldiers marching against the sands spurred him on as he directed them towards the Fields of Carcarus.

These fields were once host to a battle between Sudra and Dura. A skirmish lasting six days, with thousands slain and ramifications lasting decades. It had been glorious. He could still taste the bloodshed.

Today they would debut another momentous event. Of that Drazah was certain.

For Drazah, summer usually meant tournaments in the coliseum. He would sit with his queen and sons, pride of place, as gladiators faced off against each other in spectacular displays of strength and agility. Rarely did he ever join in himself, but on occasion, an over-confident buffoon would challenge him for the crown, and he would get to stretch his wings a little.

However, over the last few months, tension between Sudra and the Empire had been rising. Drazah had been beginning to fear invasion when a Duran messenger arrived. The message invited him to meet the emperor on the battlefields of their ancestors to negotiate an alliance between Sudra and the newly formed Duran Empire.

Drazah didn't think it necessary, but Nymati was insistent on him taking as many men as he could manage, keeping up appearances as always. Each of his one thousand men were given a sword and shield, but as they didn't have the supplies to clothe them all, most wore only parts of the full uniform. They looked ridiculous, but two children and twenty years was hardly the time to wait before questioning his queen.

He reined in his elephant, taking in the view of the battlefield. Tents with red roofs were propped up all over the fields. There were pens holding horses, carts filled with supplies, and campfires surrounded by waiting soldiers. The army boasted tens of thousands of bronze-clad soldiers covering the landscape, the sheer volume of them making Drazah's single battalion seem rather feeble. Even at a distance, he could spot the Estra among their ranks, their horse bodies raising their torsos above the Dura.

Drazah could only hope their reputation deterred any ideas the emperor had of attacking his meagre forces head-on. The might of a fully powered Sudra was legendary.

After all, the emperor didn't know their secret.

* * *

Drazah dismounted, meeting the emperor with confidence.

"I didn't expect you to bring your entire army for a simple negotiation, Gabris," Drazah chided, feigning amazement. Having received word by crow, he was unsurprised at the display, but would have expected as much regardless.

"Fear not, Drazah, I thought it only right I show you what I was offering," replied the emperor as he gestured over the masses of soldiers around them.

Emperor Callius Gabris was a demi-god of a man. He stood over a foot taller than most of his Duran soldiers, a giant in every sense of the word, his muscles hulking out from under his armour. On his chest, he sported a polished bronze chest-plate, embellished with an extraordinary amount of muscles, and his once peachy complexion glowed bronze in the sun. Upon his head, he wore a brightly polished bronze galea which came down over his cheeks, framing his square face to highlight piercing violet eyes.

"Oh? And what is it that you're offering?" Drazah raised a single, sceptical eyebrow.

The emperor smirked his response. He continued to walk them down along the frontline. His thick crimson cape draped from his shoulders to drag on the ground behind him - where the golden embroidery glittered in the sun.

"To be a part of something bigger than yourself. The chance to save your people from poverty."

The emperor spoke profoundly, but Drazah thought him no more convincing than a two-bit salesman; cocky, desperate and peddling false promises.

"And what would you have in return?"

"Bend the knee," stated the emperor, thick leather bracer's clinging to his wrists as he extended his muscular arm. "Become the fourth country of the great Duran Empire. With your men in my army, I would be unstoppable, and-"

"I cannot allow you to force my men to fight a war that is not theirs," Drazah warned. He tried to hide his eagerness, but could not allow the emperor to continue.

"You say that as if you have a choice..." The emperor sneered, his helm dropping with his brow. "Your people were once one of the greatest in the whole of Alamantra. I can make them great again. With or without you."

"You dare threaten me?" Drazah raised his voice, a growl licking his lips as his tail flicked behind him.

"The choice is yours, Drazah," The emperor shrugged. "You can swallow your pride and do what's best for your people. Or you can resist, and watch as my army marches across your lands. Slaughtering any and all who resist us."

Drazah's jaw set as he stared down the emperor. His people were in no position to face such an impressive army, there was no way they could win any kind of battle. He had always known this, however, he was not willing to give up his kingdom just yet.

The whole journey he had thought about it. His mind was set, his body ready.

He knew what he had to do.

"You may think you have me at a disadvantage, Callius, but I will not go down without a fight," Drazah challenged. "However, I have no intention of shedding the blood of my men over your foolish quest to polish your ego."

Drazah burned with fury. The emperor's arrogance made him sick. He was immature and cocky. He was brazen beyond measure. He was everything Drazah despised in a man, but his bravado would be his downfall.

"If you want my kingdom you will have to take it yourself," Drazah blelted out. "Right here. Right now. For all our men to see. A king's wager, you and I. Here on the battlefield of our ancestors." Drazah pulled on his sword, a khopesh forged from an obsidian black metal which gleamed in the sun, and aimed it towards the emperor.

"I challenge you to a DUEL."

Silence erupted through the camp as soldiers on both sides stood with gaping mouths, waiting for the emperor's response. Although, none were expecting what happened next.

The emperor laughed, although due to his general size it was closer to a bellow. "You've got guts, old man, but I hold all the cards. I'll give you one chance to rescind your challenge."

The mockery only fuelled the inferno growing within Drazah, but only his nostrils flared as he glared down his opponent. The emperor could spout all the drivel he wanted, Drazah had no intention of backing down now.

This was the only way it could go. Drazah knew from the moment he received the summons - *before even*.

The emperor was merely an overzealous bully, relying

on brute force to overpower his enemies. The tactic may have worked on weaker nations, but not Sudra. Not Drazah.

Sudra was at a disadvantage, that much was true, but one-on-one the emperor's size and confidence would be his undoing. One-on-one, Drazah would take the advantage, steal a quick victory and make his queen proud.

Drazah's grip tightened around his khopesh. He tilted its sharp blade just enough to reiterate his threat, his tail held straight behind him.

The emperor sucked his teeth. "Very well, state your terms."

"You win, my men march you back to the capital where my queen will surrender, peacefully. I win, no more Empire and your men all go home," roared Drazah, his khopesh still firmly pointed at the emperor.

The emperor threw off the cape hugging his shoulders, unsheathing his broadsword in a single, swift, one-handed movement. It was unlike any broadsword Drazah had ever seen. A thick blade of polished steel, a full foot and a half longer than a standard broadsword and easily a foot wide, the hilt glistening with bright gold. A lesser man would have strained under its weight, but the emperor held the beastly sword with pride and grace.

"Clear space," boomed the emperor, his voice echoing around the nervous onlookers.

As instructed, anyone within twenty metres snapped to attention and cleared the field. Only the rustle of boots on dry sandy grass and the clink of armour broke the silence, as foot soldiers hurried out of the way. Both armies merged into a huddled mass, creating a ring around their leaders.

The emperor rolled his heavy shoulders as he readied himself. Feet firmly on the ground, he squared off his body, casually twisting the giant broadsword around to affirm his grip.

Drazah had yet to move a muscle. Inside, he was shaking, a battle lust surging through his muscles as his body prepared for the battle to come.

'This is the only way,' he told himself. *'Only I can save my people now.'*

The quiet before a fight was the only sensation he could ever equate to the moment before his queen fed on him.

The familiar energy rose rapidly within. He thought of her then as he reminded himself of all he was fighting for. He reminded himself of his people and the vow he made to protect them and their secret. He thought of his men and the war they would be forced to fight should he fail in his task. And lastly, his thoughts turned to his sons, whom he wished he'd brought with him so they could watch as history was made before their very eyes.

One way or another.

* * *

CHAPTER THREE

Thanks to her shift change, Reyla was up early to take the princess to visit twin nobles Lierin and Tierin.

It was already warm as she left the barracks and crossed the grounds to the palace. She swept the quiet corridors to the princess' room.

Nasir gave Reyla a wry smile as she arrived, likely hoping to gauge if she harboured any resentment for making her take his shift. He received only a nod in return as Reyla passed by, unwilling to let him off the hook so easily.

She wouldn't say anything, but Reyla was furious her shift had been changed at the last minute, yet again. It was an all too regular occurrence. As the only woman on the Palace Guard, she was often given guard of social events, but she was used to it. She was the only female soldier in the whole Freya Army, the other women (*there were seven in total*) having become medics.

Being the only woman in the Freya Army was never as much of an issue for Reyla as it was for others. She was sixteen when she decided on her dream of becoming a knight - and once she had been given the chance she was not going to let anything stop her. Save perhaps being arrested for sneaking around with the princess, but she would fell that tree if it came to it.

Arafrey was already dressed and sitting with a finished breakfast plate, waiting for her. She turned to Reyla as Ceal cleaned away her crockery, her emerald eyes shining the greeting they so longed to give each other.

"Ready?"

"Suppose," grumbled the princess, her glimmer quickly fading.

It was only a short distance to the twins' house, so they walked, cutting through the market on their way toward the noble district.

Although the previous night left a substantial longing deep within her, Reyla was the height of professionalism. She walked a few feet behind Arafrey, far enough to guard efficiently but still close enough to smell her lavender fragrance.

Arafrey always smelt of lavender. Reyla made the perfume herself using her artes upon wildflowers. She had quite a talent for this, yet she lacked the proficiency others had with healing artes.

Reyla scanned the market, eyeballing the patrons as they passed by. Daring them to test her.

While the Frey were known for their sagely robes and flowing attire, these were often expensive and wildly impractical for traversing the forests. As such, only those of noble birth tended to wear them, and many of the Frey around them wore tighter-fitting leaf-leather garbs with tunics or smocks, a sure sign of their working-class status.

The aroma of fresh herbs and flowers breezed through the market, carrying with it the distant sounds of a flute coming from the Cross Road Pavilion. This was soon overpowered by earthy undertones from mountains of succulent fruits and vegetables piled on to the wooden stalls.

The markets were always busy this time of the morning. The merchants called out to the passers-by in hopes of a sale, an ever-present droning that swallowed most other sounds. Reyla noticed Night-Shift Guards from the palace, trying to stay awake long enough to do their shopping before dragging themselves back to the barracks. Others looked like the staff of noble houses collecting the groceries of their employers, or nattering housewives who had nothing better to do than gossip and ignore their children all day.

Arafrey turned over her shoulder as they passed by the flower stall. She half smiled to Reyla, the smell of fresh lavender joining them in a secret moment of intimacy, before she carried on.

It pained Reyla to have to walk in silence through the busy market; the distance between the secret lovers serving as a strong reminder of what could never be. She longed for the day she would be able to take Arafrey's hand in hers and walk along the street. A day where they didn't have to hide their feelings. A day where she didn't have to lie. But she knew that day would never come.

Even then, she chastised herself for stealing the occasional glance of Arafrey's rear in her fitted cream robes – but it was quite alluring…

They turned on to Avenall road going east toward the Life Tree. Fancy boutiques with overpriced clothes and ornaments favoured by the noble Frey framed their path as they continued heading towards the noble district. The boutiques were grown from trees, formed with artes to incorporate them into the structure of the building. Many of them boasted imported glass for grand display windows, where exquisite and ridiculously expensive robes were proudly displayed.

The noble district also housed the city temple, a magnificent building grown from the roots of the Life Tree. Here, the Life Tree's thick body stretched far beyond the canopy above them, the Manastream flowing through it showering them with a soft luminescence at all times.

They arrived at the home of Lierin and Tierin, a lavish building grown from oak with flowerbeds of bluebells framing a stepping stone path. Arafrey rang the doorbell, looking to Reyla as each hoped no one would answer.

Much to their dismay, a young woman in a white apron soon answered the door. She guided them through the wooden halls and out into the rear garden where the twins awaited them.

"Oh, Ara! We were just about to send out a search party," Lierin sneered, her nose in the air. "Do sit down."

Reyla ducked away to begin her sweep before catching the twins' attention, leaving Arafrey exchanging pleasantries.

"I do apologise, we cut through the market on the way here and it was dreadfully busy," said Arafrey. Reyla tried not to listen; she didn't like how the princess changed to suit those around her.

The princess didn't like the twins all that much, but their father was a prominent politician, and they grew up in the same social circles. The pair peacocked their noble status, often draped in luxurious fabrics and doused in overpowering perfumes with their flat noses held high in permanent entitlement.

"Why bother yourself with the market, Ara?" asked Lierin, the informal use of the princess' name grinding against the mortar of Reyla's patience.

The twins always wore matching dresses with many layers, this time in a soft blue. Their drab hair was woven into intricate braids that raised above their heads, making them seem taller than they were. Few Frey wore make-up of any kind, but they had an unnatural paleness to their face and a rouge about their cheeks suggesting they did.

Reyla thought perhaps their flashy clothes and hair were there to distract from the plainness of the twin's features and foul personalities. It didn't.

The three women continued gossiping while Reyla finished her sweep of the manicured garden, setting herself with her back to the wall and a clear view of the table. She half-listened in to the conversation, but it was like an arrow to the heart when the topic inevitably turned to the subject of *men*.

"What about you, Ara? Who're you taking to the festival? Tierin still hasn't been asked by anyone." Lierin spoke at speed, often forgetting to pause for breath.

Tierin bobbed her head in silent agreement. Although

both twins were well-spoken, Tierin often fell quiet and let her sister speak for her, not that she had much choice in the matter.

"I hadn't thought about it." Arafrey spoke quietly, before attempting in vain to change the subject.

Of course, she had thought about it. Arafrey thought about it a lot, but the princess would rather go alone than have to spend the night pretending to like some noble hoping to win her affection. She tried to play along with her parent's wishes and do what was expected of her, but Arafrey always felt guilty about leading her suitors on.

"Well, you can't go alone, that would be horrible. And you can't go with just anyone."

Arafrey ignored her. She collected a spoon off the table and stirred her green tea before lifting it to her lips.

"I heard Bodair is taking some commoner friend of his," Lierin continued without prompting. "Can you even imagine?"

Arafrey rolled her eyes. "It's really not that big of a deal. She's a childhood friend."

"What kind of a noble, high-born would want to marry him after he's been dating a *pig*?"

Although it made Reyla's blood boil, *'pig'* was a frequently used slang name the upper class used to describe those less fortunate than themselves.

"Don't be so dramatic," Arafrey huffed, fighting her frustration. She hated the way her friends spoke about her people as if they were garbage because they were not noble-born. The class divide in Freya was so minuscule the princess thought it asinine to place so much value in it. Just being noble-born didn't make them a good Frey; *the twins were proof of that.*

"I don't know, our father said I was to avoid him now."

"Social suicide," Tierin finally whispered.

"Whatever. Why would I want a husband who was so shallow and superficial they cared who my *ex* was?" Arafrey shook her head, the strain evident in her voice as she tired of the conversation.

"And where do you intend to find a high-born who isn't like that?" joked Lierin. The three Frey all laughed together, breaking Arafrey's frustration, before they carried on with their conversation.

Reyla meanwhile remained quietly at her post, trying hard not to listen in, but she had not done well.

She had always known there would be trouble if their relationship were ever exposed, but it became ever apparent in that moment that she had sorely miscalculated the potential fallout.

Before, Reyla told herself their actions were victimless, that it was just an outdated belief. She consoled herself with the knowledge that she would bear the brunt of the blame, but as she listened to the twins spouting off their elitist drivel, she realised that was not the case. Reyla's perfect princess would never be so crass as to judge a person by their blood, or past relations, but all of a sudden, she was brutally reminded it was not the same with all Frey.

Panic came over her like a wave. A weight pressed down upon her shoulders as some unseen force wrapped around her chest. Her knees trembled, threatening to give way as she desperately fought the instincts screaming at her to run.

Reyla cursed herself. Until that very moment, she had never once considered Arafrey's reputation or how it would affect who would inevitably become King of Freya. After all, why would she? What reputation did she have to consider?

It was as if someone shook her awake, and the full extent of her selfish and repugnant actions were too much for her stomach to bear.

Reyla swallowed the bile residing in her throat. Taking a long breath, her hand tightened around her shield, as she tried to maintain the illusion of composure. She always thought herself a loyal, model citizen, but now she wasn't so sure. Was she so concerned with betraying Frey beliefs that she hadn't considered the possibility she was betraying her kingdom? Or did she just choose not to think about it?

Reyla focused her attention in an attempt to stop her head from spinning. Staring at a purple and white lily, she watched as a bumblebee hovered around the flower, teetering around the petals a while before floating off. *How she wished she could follow it.*

Reyla drew another deep breath. Her hand shook, but she was doing okay. Standing there would be the easy part. It's what she had to do next that would be the hardest of all.

She just had to make it through the rest of her shift.

* * *

A gentle breeze tussled through the leaves of the Life Tree above them as Elsafrey filled a small bowl with water from the manapool. She crossed the temple courtyard to an elderly man who sat uneasily among the wooden pews. He grasped at his chest, wailing in pain.

Elsafrey soaked a cloth in the bowl and dabbed the man's forehead. The poor old Frey had black marks on his skin across his face and arms. Although the marks seemed to appear on their own, they dug into the skin, making it blister and crease at the edges, almost like burns.

As the High Priestess of Freya, it was Elsafrey's job to tend to the well-being of her people. She tended their physical health with healing artes and medicine and tended their spiritual needs through prayer and by passing on the many teachings of Auldafrey, the first of their kind.

Elsafrey smiled at the old Frey reassuringly, gently stroking his hair before excusing herself and catching the attention of a medic.

"Sister Alma. He's the fourth to come in with these symptoms this morning," she whispered, looking around to make sure no one was listening in. "I'm worried we have a sickness on our hands. Could you check those waiting and separate those with these symptoms from those without who need treatment? It may be contagious."

"Yes, Ma'am. It's just…" the worried medic trailed off,

looking to the Priestess with wide eyes. "I already have, your Grace, they're all affected…"

Elsafrey scanned the temple, counting the number of Frey sitting in the pews. Bile rippled through her stomach, churning as she realised the number of patients was much higher than normal. Her eyes darted between the patients, scanning them urgently for one who was not showing the symptoms.

"Quarantine the temple," Elsafrey instructed. "I must speak with the king."

* * *

CHAPTER FOUR

Drazah calmed his nerves, focusing on his opponent.

"It doesn't have to be this way, Drazah," called the emperor. "Would it be so bad to bend the knee and pass the reins to a better man?"

"I'll let you know when one offers," boomed Drazah, diving swiftly forward toward the emperor, his khopesh outstretched ahead of him.

Drazah moved with the speed of a sandstorm at its peak. He thrust his slender khopesh with incredible strength and uncanny agility, but each thrust he threw was knocked to the side with ease as it careened along the flat of the giant broadsword. The massive blade met each attack with calm precision. For every parry, the king was ready with another jab, only to be blocked effortlessly by the emperor. Looking for an opening, Drazah's feet never stopped as he danced around the emperor, but try as he might, he was unable to wound or even strike the barbaric figure.

The emperor swung his broadsword, the air wailing as the weight of the blade cut through with unnatural speed. Drazah was quick too, he ducked reflexively to avoid the monolithic weapon, bringing his khopesh up into the emperor's stomach. The black steel screeched against the bronze chest-plate as it deflected harmlessly away.

The Sudran king rallied but the emperor knocked back yet another attack, and another, his eyes catching Drazah's for the briefest moment. They glared back, ultraviolet and alive with exhilaration. A smirk stretched past the side of the emperor's galea as he looked to Drazah, defending one more thrust without breaking their connection.

Drazah hissed. The emperor was enjoying their performance.

Drazah was tiring, but his opponent had barely drawn a sweat. He couldn't believe how fast the bulging mass of muscles standing before him shifted. It was as if he moved in slow motion as the emperor casually deflected his khopesh. Clearly, it was time to change his approach.

As he expected, Drazah's attack was foiled once more. He followed through into an evasive roll, coming back up to face the emperor to the outside of their clearing.

"Are you going to get serious?" laughed the emperor.

Drazah snarled in response, his face scrunched as he threw his khopesh to the ground and called to the power hiding within his core. His tail coiled and flicked as something called back from deep within. It had been so long since he last transformed, he was almost excited.

The Sudran King lifted his head and released a mighty roar, willing his body into action. His heart pounded against his chest, sending the blood *billowing* through his body, as he activated his artes, and his mana surged.

First came his wings, the skin ripping as they erupted from his back and fanned out behind him. The adrenaline rushed through his body, drumming against his ears as his wings stretched out to full span, and his muscles bulged. His nails expanded into sharp, white claws. His horns extended into a point, turning with the rest of his body as his skin darkened - becoming jet black. Drazah affirmed his stance and presented his true form, a demonic creature over eight feet in height that would have been imposing to anyone other than his current opponent.

Drazah tore away his ripped clothing, his fury focusing as his eyes set on the emperor. His mouth foamed. *This time he wouldn't hold back.*

Drazah didn't give anyone the chance to admire his fully realised form before he drove forward with newfound aggression and blinding speed.

In less than a blink, the emperor readied his sword.

Drazah came in hard with his right fist. Then his left. The speed of his demon form forced the emperor to work harder to dodge his attacks, but still, that colossal sword blocked him.

The emperor sidestepped deftly, using his unique blade's width in place of a shield, becoming an incredible hybrid weapon in his hands. It allowed the emperor to casually brush off Drazah's attacks, and any time there was an opening the emperor's strength and incredible speed pulled the hulking broadsword around to meet any incoming attack.

Drazah ripped his claws towards the emperor, screeching them across the metal with a flare of sparks as he failed to break through the emperor's defences. The Sudran tried again, batting his wings continuously, whipping great gusts of wind at the emperor to little effect. Drazah's flight added weight to his movements as he swung his arms around with frenzied force. Blow after hammering blow.

The attacks came in fast and repeatedly. Drazah used his wings to lift around the emperor with ease, staying evasive while putting his whole weight behind each strike. Harried, the emperor could only use his sword to defend as Drazah continued his assault. However, the Demon King had yet to land a single damaging blow as each powerful claw glanced off armour and sword alike, his frustration building with every second.

Sweat dripped off Drazah's brow, tracing his eye. He blinked it away, and in an instant, his guard was down.

The emperor made use of the opening, slamming the flat of his sword directly into Drazah, who rolled into it, spreading the impact across his shoulder. The force echoed through his arm, sending a wave of pins and needles shooting through to his fingertips.

The blow caused Drazah to slide to the side. He spread his hand wide against the sandy grass to maintain his balance. A firm flap of his wings held Drazah steady as he slowed, the sand wrapping a cloud of dust around them.

As he came to a stop, Drazah's fingers brushed against the familiar cool metal of his khopesh. It was tiny in his demon claw. He grasped it tightly as he dived in for one final assault.

This was it. He could feel it. It was now or never.

Drazah bolted forward with all his might, every last ounce of strength in his legs and wings pushing him forward. Black khopesh held firm and proud, he lunged towards the emperor. Fury raged, scalding pressure urging him forward, erupting like a geyser, as his blade finally hit skin. He revelled in his victory, blood spraying over the emperor as Drazah stared him down. His body burned in righteous victory.

Drazah halted. Shocked.

Although he landed his khopesh, it hardly glanced across the emperor's shoulder as he turned and sunk his blade deep into Drazah's belly.

The emperor swung his blade with such force it sliced through the king's side, left to right as if it was butter until it stuck hard in splintered bone.

Drazah released a gut-curdling roar that trailed off into a weak gurgle. His hulking demon body doubled over. He coughed, blood streaking down his chin, as he grabbed at the wound in horror.

Did he fail?

Drazah turned cold as blood drained from his body. A wave of fear and regret washed over him as he realised himself. His knees buckled, unable to hold the weight of his failure and guilt. Blood pooling in the sand around his knees, the broadsword stuck firm as he slowly reverted to his lesser form.

The surrounding soldiers stood silent.

They watched as the emperor placed his foot on

Drazah's chest, bracing as he pulled out his now blood-soaked sword. He whipped it to the side, casting splatter along the ground. Drazah's sight grew dark as the emperor walked away.

"Raltz! Ready the troops," ordered the emperor, not bothering to look back as he wiped down his blade.

"We're moving out!"

* * *

Queen Nymati was in the library, looking east through an open window when it happened.

With a sudden beat, her heart thumped as if trying to burst through her chest. A pulse tore through her entire body, a wave of savage pain catching her breath and ripping right through to her soul. Tears welled in her ruby eyes as she stared unblinking into the desert horizon. Her body was shocked into dysfunction as Drazah breathed his last, shattering their parabond.

Nymati grasped her chest in horror.

It was a pain like no other. She grew so hollow that her trembling heart rattled in her chest, every beat excruciating, strenuous. A river of tears to rival the Ballish streamed down her cheeks as she crumpled to the ground, crying without sound.

It had been mere moments, but to Nymati that moment was never-ending.

She lay on the sandstone floor, tears pooling on the

bridge of her nose before overflowing. Mind, body and soul exhausted, it was all she could do to keep breathing, as a dark silence took over her heart, drowning her in despair.

Nymati had heard how painful breaking a parabond was, but always considered it an exaggeration. Having shrugged off the labours of childbirth despite the many horror stories, she always assumed losing Drazah would be likewise, *but this*? This was beyond anything Nymati ever imagined. Malaki near floated out the womb in comparison.

She gnawed her tongue against her fangs as if to wake herself from a terrible nightmare. Perhaps her arrogance would be the end of them both, but she felt it no more than she deserved.

Nymati became aware of a crowd forming around her and the sounds of her eldest son pushing his way through. He scooped her off the floor and into his arms, drawing her close. She caught a glimpse of his azure eyes and umber hair, and turned away. Squeezing away the last of her tears, she buried her head in his chest, unable to bear the resemblance to her dear darling Drazah.

Her chest heaved with every breath, her eyes remained tight shut as Amynus stroked her hair, rocking gently back and forth. She just lay there, helpless, her skin cold against his, her body frail and unable to function.

Amynus climbed to his feet, cradling Nymati like a child and carrying her through the palace. She kept her head nestled into his chest, unaware of the distressed looks from the concerned citizens they passed in the halls.

Nymati remained lifeless as Amynus placed her with her head on a pillow, her eyes finally opening to find her bedroom. She lay there, her ruby eyes dull and glazed over. Her breathing so shallow, it may as well stop; her heart so broken, she feared it might.

She was never supposed to do this without him.

How could she possibly carry on?

* * *

CHAPTER FIVE

Reyla successfully maintained her composure for the rest of her shift, but it was a task.

Returning to the palace offered her little relief. Their usual silence taunted her with frenzied thoughts as she searched for a way to repent her sins. She had to fix things before it was too late. Before their secret was found out.

Her heart hadn't stopped racing since the twins'. Her senses continued to scream as her anxiety raged on, ready to burst forth at any moment; every breath she took more despicable than the last.

Reyla hated herself.

How could she be so selfish?

How did she not see?

They arrived at Arafrey's bedroom, her usual anticipation replaced with a pang of sickening guilt. It tore her insides apart.

Unaware, Arafrey closed the door behind them with gusto and threw her arms around Reyla.

"We have some time before your shift ends," she purred, a wide smile over her blushing cheeks. Arafrey's hands were like silk, brushing over Reyla as she pulled in close, placing a soft kiss on her green lips.

Reyla held her tongue, her thoughts too grievous to share. Her eyes fell empty as Arafrey pulled at her armour. Her heart cold, she swallowed. *It was now or never.*

Reyla stopped Arafrey. Her fingers wrapped around the princess' delicate wrists as she held Arafrey still, her grasp feeble.

"Princess... I... We..." Reyla forced out a whisper, eyes to the floor. Her strength quickly failing, she searched for the correct words to say.

"Reyla?" Arafrey's voice wavered with uncertainty; already she suspected something was wrong.

"My princess, I will always protect you, but I..." Reyla paused, catching her breath as each word ripped through her like a dagger. "I always knew we could never... And if we were found out..."

Reyla had never been good with words. Give her any other task and she would surely excel. But feelings were hard for her to convey. It wasn't that she didn't feel these things, more that she had never expressed them before, or that she had spent most of her time trying to suppress them. Between working in the castle and joining the army, she never really had time to figure that kind of thing out. It wasn't like she had many friends to talk to either. All she ever had was her princess, which made things so much harder.

She tightened her hand. "I didn't care. I was willing to risk it all to be with you."

"But Reyla, I l-"

"Ara, please..." she burst out, pushing the princess away. "This whole time I was so busy not caring what would happen to me; when I should've been worried about what would happen to you."

"You-" The princess hesitated at the use of her name. "You can't listen to those girls. They were just gossiping!"

"But they were right," Reyla snapped. "Like it or not, you *are* the princess, and you have your role to play in this kingdom's future."

Reyla tried not to look away as tears bubbled in Arafrey's emerald eyes. Each tremble of her perfect juniper lips was like a gut-punch but Reyla made up her mind. She was doing the right thing, she was certain. She couldn't afford to lose her resolve now.

"Please, Reyla," Arafrey sobbed, although Reyla suspected she very much wanted to scream the palace down.

"I'm serious this time," Reyla asserted, finally managing to hold eye contact, her face set, determined despite the pain in her chest. "It's time we accept that role doesn't... *can't*... involve me..."

Tears streamed down Arafrey's face as Reyla turned to leave.

"Please... don't do this..."

* * *

Reyla trudged towards the barracks, replaying her

conversation with the princess in her mind. Her body ran heavy yet empty, every step leading her away from the princess' bedroom growing harder than the last.

She hesitated, her eyes to the floor as her feet threatened to turn.

If she ran back, maybe they could come up with a plan. Maybe they could run away together as they had always dreamed. They could run, never look back, live off the lands in peace and-

No.

No, she was doing the right thing.

She was certain.

Reyla's internal struggle continued as she walked. The muscles in her back tightened to form one giant knot as she curled deeper into herself.

Soul tortured. Heart still.

"REEEEEEEYLA!"

Reyla was so wrapped up in her quandary, she failed to notice the excited yelling following her.

"Hey! Reyla!"

She flinched as the voice brought her back to the barracks where a young Frey ran up to her. They wore the same uniform, but his held the red cloak and motifs of the Queen's Guard.

"Hey, Tharin. What's up?"

The youngest of three sons, Tharin Berrin was a charismatic Frey, with eyes a perennial blue and cheek dimples you could stick your thumbs in whenever he smiled. Tharin was on the Princess' Guard when Reyla first received her promotion, and they became fast friends despite his noble background. He wore his hair short like the common Frey on the Guard, a caramel blonde that sprang from the right into an impossibly tidy fringe.

"You'll never guess," Tharin raved, overly excited, even for him. "So. There I am, on duty, right. Then all these sick guys start showing up out of nowhere…"

Despite his noble heritage, Tharin spent a lot of time with the commoners on the Palace Guard, and as such his vocabulary was often at odds with his posher accent. The local women seemed to like it as Tharin was usually found with a gaggle of girls fawning over him in the local tavern, much to the displeasure of his girlfriend. He had calmed down over recent years though and, at twenty-five, talked of settling down. However, Reyla was sure he would always be the same goofball.

"…and then the queen turns to Mika and is like." He changed his voice to do a poor impression. "*We need additional guards during this crisis.*" He continued in his own voice, "and then the queen hands him this list and tells him everyone on it is to be reassigned immediately to the Queen's Guard as of tomorrow. And do you know whose name was on the top of that list?"

"No, why don't you tell me?" asked Reyla, fast growing tired of her friends' rambling.

"It. Was. You."

"Oh?"

She frowned. She heard what he said, but it didn't register. *Was that good news?*

"Come on, that's awesome! We get to be on duty together." He grinned. "I even wrangled us the first night shift! Will be just like old times!"

He grabbed Reyla into a hug, tussling her shaggy mane. She slunk out of her depression enough to give him a forced smile and laugh.

"Let's go to the Hill's Tavern and toast your promotion! We need to get you in the proper colours too," he said, pulling on her green cape. "You can at least look like you're part of the Queen's Guard while you're here!"

Reyla touched the green sigil of the Princess' Guard on her breast. She had worked for the princess for so long that it was going to be strange wearing different colours. Perhaps it was time for her to move on.

"We need ale!" Tharin declared. "Lots of it!"

* * *

CHAPTER SIX

Amynus closed the bedroom door behind him, a strange sickness bubbling within his stomach.

He had never seen his mother cry before. It was strange to see her so vulnerable, so weak. He wasn't quite sure how to feel about it. Although, he wasn't sure how to feel about a fair number of things at that particular moment. He was sad and proud, also worried and resentful, but more than anything he was angry - so very, very angry.

In Sudra, it was the greatest honour to die protecting your kingdom, but to fall at the hand of a Duran? And a single Duran at that?

Amynus could only imagine what a man this Emperor must be to have defeated the great Drazah.

"How is she?" came a brittle voice.

Amynus looked up to find the stony eyes of Aeryn, the head of his mother's staff. He supposed she had been waiting out there this whole time.

"Not great," he admitted, considering her a meddlesome wench, but one dedicated to the crown enough to trust in this instance. "Their bond has broken. We should prepare for the emperor's arrival."

Aeryn swallowed. "And you?" she asked and Amynus scowled his response. "You need to be strong, Highness. With Her Majesty incapacitated, people will be looking to you for answers."

"Like I have any," he hissed, the sore subject poking holes in his already simmering composure. "Even if Mother has a contingency plan in place, you know I'd be the last to know."

Aeryn bowed her head in agreement, too loyal to speak poorly of her master. Amynus scoffed at her silence.

"We already have our assignments," offered Aeryn timidly. "We can continue with them until Her Majesty is feeling better."

"That's great," he replied, catching the bitterness in his tone. "Do you know when she fed last?"

Aeryn shook her head. "Should I send in the new girl?"

"No, I'm not sure she'll have the strength of restraint. See if you can tempt her with something from the dungeon before sending in someone we'll miss."

"As you wish." Aeryn bowed.

"It's essential we keep her energy levels up," Amynus warned. "I shan't lose both my parents to the will of the Empire."

Aeryn bowed once more and made her exit, leaving Amynus alone with his thoughts. Or rather, just one thought.

His hands curled into tight fists with a single, newfound desire that burned in the pit of his stomach:

Revenge.

* * *

CHAPTER SEVEN

It was cool the next evening, as Reyla and Tharin took their posts in the temple courtyard. The manapool shone mystic blue behind them, the moon peering through the trees as they watched over the sleeping patients.

"Seems like this sickness is something serious," whispered Tharin with genuine concern.

Reyla sighed in agreement while shuffling uncomfortably in her new uniform.

The number of Frey presenting symptoms of the black sickness only increased as the day went on. The temple wards filled quickly, overflowing into the courtyard. Bunks had been taken from the barracks, but they too were quickly occupied.

"What d'you think's causing it?"

"Dunno. Whatever it is, the high priestess'll have it cured in no time," Reyla assured him, looking to the starry skies. Her eyes followed the roots of the Life Tree as they curved around them and merged seamlessly into the temple walls.

"I suppose. It's just…" he trailed off, watching as one of the patients turned over in their bed.

Reyla rolled her shoulders habitually, the right cracking through the quiet. She clawed at the old injury, making a mental note to seek aid in the morning. The pain shifted, engulfing her chest, as she realised she could no longer rely on her princess for relief.

"Did you hear about Estra?" Tharin continued, choosing to discard his previous thought. "Can't believe they've joined the Dura."

Reyla abandoned her self-loathing to consider the news. She found it hard to imagine the Estra being push-overs. Their people were well known for their bravery and skill in battle. The idea they were just invaded was surreal.

"What happened?"

"Gurrein said the Empire marched on them overnight, burning everything in their path. Beating and capturing anyone they could," Tharin explained. "Apparently, all the men have been forced to join the Empires' army and cart supplies around like animals!"

"How awful."

"Well, they are half horse, aren't they? It's better than being on the menu; I hear the Dura eat anything."

"No, that's Sudra."

Tharin flashed his cheek dimples. "I only heard that about the women."

They sniggered, soon falling quiet.

It was at this moment a shadow moved in the temple corridor, catching their attention.

"Did you...?" asked Reyla, her hazel eyes darting to

the courtyard door, expecting it to open.

Tharin nodded in response, his hand reaching for his sword, each scanning the windows for the sign of movement.

"Should we?"

"Let's," affirmed Tharin, his voice unusually serious.

The two Frey drew their swords, hands tight around their shields as they stalked through the courtyard. Reyla lagged behind, allowing Tharin to take the lead as they eased the double doors open and peered inside.

Darkness filled the empty corridor, forcing Reyla to strain her senses for a sign of malicious intent.

Down the wooden corridors, the ward doors were left ajar, those behind supposedly sleeping. The glow from the Life Tree panelled through the windows to the floor running down each wing undisturbed. Two guards stood by the temple entrance and another two down the east wing by Elsafrey's office, all equally unaware of any intrusion.

Reyla scanned the corridor once more, ready to give up and return to her post when she caught a scurrying from the west. Her head snapped to the source, Tharin's too, and they set off in a jog.

The light pat of footsteps became clearer as they reached the end of the corridor, where a door lay open. As they approached, a musty breeze brushed past the frame from the catacombs below, bringing with it more footsteps.

"In here," Tharin urged, holding the door for her to go first. He out-ranked Reyla, but had yet to develop her backbone.

Reyla rolled her shoulder as she passed by him. Stone steps led down into the labyrinth below, the dry air warmed by the glow of the Life Tree's roots marbling the walls around them.

"You ever been down here?" Reyla whispered, tiptoeing around ornaments left in tribute to their fallen leaders. The catacombs were kept immaculately clean otherwise, the many tombstones of Frey royal ancestors lining the walls tended with care.

Tharin returned a big cheesy grin and turned his thumb up. "I don't think we're allowed to be here!"

Reyla grimaced. "Let's just check this out and get out of here before anyone notices."

As they continued down the path, a low chanting came from the area ahead, soon followed by menacing lights that flashed up the passage. Reyla lifted her hand, slowing their pace as each tightened their grip around sword and shield. With their backs pressed against the wall, they stole a glance at the origin. A cloaked figure held their hands against the soil wall, chanting as they activated strange dark purple artes.

"Gar Veen Tier Metra."

It was a soft, feminine voice, but not a language Reyla recognised.

Reyla turned back to Tharin, he frowned, inclining his head to the figure. She lifted her chin, offering to follow his lead as the two Frey leapt into action, swords aimed at the cloaked stranger.

"Stop right there! You… creepy… weird… Person!" shouted Tharin, having lost his train of thought once his mouth opened.

Reyla shot him a look before turning back to the cloaked figure. "What're you doing here?"

The figure ignored them. They activated their artes, putrid dark purple mana surrounding their fists as they raised their arms.

"Perictara!"

A flash of light filled the passage, soon followed by smoke.

Reyla ignored the display, launching forward with Tharin beside her, but the cloaked figure had already vanished. With nothing to attack, the two Frey followed through and crashed into the side of the passage, taking several ornaments with them.

Each bounced back at the ready, but there was no sign of the cloaked figure.

As the smoke cleared, they brushed the dirt and shards of broken ceramics off their clothes. Reyla combed her hands through her dusty hair, and examined the wall before them. It was ordinary enough, except for a knot in the tree roots about the size of an apple. She studied the knot more closely, pushing it a few times.

"I wonder what they were doing," mused Reyla. She stepped back, half hoping there would be a delayed reaction, but nothing happened.

"Who knows?" Tharin shrugged, his face twisting in anguish to see the mess they had made. "Oh, man! We're going to be in so much trouble!"

"It's not like we can keep this a secret," Reyla scolded. "What if they're the one causing the sickness? We have to do something."

"I know, I know. It's just..." he whined, his voice cracking as tears threatened. "I bet that vase was really expensive, priceless even! Y'know they're going to dock it out of my pay!"

Tharin was beside himself and in the throes of a full-on meltdown, when a light glowed in the middle of the wall. Reyla shielded her eyes as the light grew stronger, with more defined edges as something formed in the centre.

She squinted her eyes as the light grew, looking closer as a burning sigil appeared in the centre. It was like a butterfly, a circle lying where the head would be, an elongated diamond centre stretched beneath it with a single teardrop wing on either side.

The light grew brighter, expanding to engulf the wall. It filled the passage with a blinding light before fading, leaving behind a white stone door. The same butterfly sigil was now embossed into the stone in gold.

Reyla held still, unsure what she saw was really there. Was this what the figure was searching for? How did they know it was there? And, most importantly, what lay on the other side?

"Should we?" asked Tharin, his hand reaching for the golden door handle.

"Yeah, let's."

The pair drew deep breaths as the door swung inwards, revealing a small room, its walls streaked with the glowing roots of the Life Tree.

It was damp and stale inside. Thick dusty cobwebs covered the ceiling, and the walls were dark and uneven. A circular stone feature dominated the floor, the painted motifs long faded and indistinguishable.

"Is this it?" asked Tharin, wandering further into the room.

Reyla followed, her footsteps echoing as they stepped on to the stone feature.

'Since when does stone echo?' she wondered as a mechanism clunked into action.

Reyla's stomach pushed into her lungs as the stone feature opened beneath them. The ground swallowed them whole as they dropped deeper underground.

The wind was knocked from her body as the two Frey thumped into the ground below. Coughing and spluttering, they rolled from the mess of leaves and branches which caught them.

"You alright?" asked Tharin, brushing himself down. He stopped suddenly, his eyes wide and sparkling. "Wow! What is this place?"

Reyla turned to find a cavern. Damp moss-covered soil made the walls, but the air was cool and fresh. The glowing roots of the Life Tree breached the ceiling and walls, cradling a pool of luminous water similar to the one in the courtyard above.

They inched toward the pool, the grass and flowers

underfoot growing thicker as they drew in closer. As they approached, a thin mist formed over the surface, where it gathered, swirling upwards. It continued to collect and expand like a lumpy typhoon until it formed a humanoid shape and features appeared.

From the mist came the image of an old Frey. Still mildly transparent, he hovered above the pool, a halo of white hair wrapping behind his pointed ears. It was uncommon for Frey to have facial hair, but this one had a long white beard that reached to his knees.

"Welcome, young Frey," said the spirit, his voice soft but deep in wisdom, "I am Auldafrey, the first of our kind."

Reyla dropped to her knees, bowing her head with Tharin beside her.

"Where are we?" she asked.

"We are deep within the bowels of the Life Tree. Beyond this chamber, the Manastream rages around us and into the tree itself," he said gesturing to the walls. "When I died my body became one with the Life Tree, so even in death I could watch over my kin. And I have been watching you, Reyla and Tharin."

"Well, that's not creepy at all," Tharin whispered to Reyla. She glared in response.

"Tharin Berrin, the noble with a common tongue. Reyla Fenwilt, the guard with a heart of roses. It was no mere coincidence you happened upon my shrine this evening.

"The sickness ravaging our lands is only the start of

what is to come. Even now, witches poison the Manastream through shrines just like mine, scattered throughout Alamantra. At the current rate, the Manastream will be completely corrupted within a matter of years, sooner if they gain access to any more shrines.

"I opened my door to you to beg, please, stop them from sending any more poison into the Manastream. We must protect the Manastream at all costs!"

"And that will cure the sickness?" asked Reyla.

"No... It will not..." admitted Auldafrey, his ghostly eyes dropping to the floor. "The sickness comes from dark-mana seeping into the stream. It's corrupting their very essence, destroying their bodies from within. I'm afraid this isn't a sickness you can just heal away. And I'm sorry, but it is not going to get better either."

"Isn't there at least something you can do?" pleaded Tharin.

"All I can do is protect the Life Tree and pray that in time the Manastream will be able to heal itself."

Reyla and Tharin shared a look between them.

"So, we stop the witches," stated Reyla, unsure as she arranged her mental inventory. She made it sound so easy.

"Well yeah, but... what's the point? You heard him, the damage is already done. There's nothing we can do..." Tharin trailed off, the pair considering the hopelessness of their situation.

"Well now, that isn't exactly true," corrected the spirit. "I said there was nothing *I* could do."

"But there's something we can do?" asked Tharin, his face lighting up.

"Perhaps…" Auldafrey tilted his head, eyeing them each in turn, Tharin eager, Reyla primed as they awaited their orders.

"Very well," said the old Frey, nodding his balding head. "When the Gods created our planet, they gave it life and sentience. Its thoughts and being flow through Alamantra as the Manastream. However, our Mother feared the planet would grow lonely on its own, so she gifted it ten of her children to keep it company. One for each of the points where the Manastream touched the surface.

"The Life Tree resides on one of these points."

Reyla looked to the roots of the Life Tree growing around them. She wondered if that was the reason the tree grew so big, but had little time to ponder as Auldafrey continued.

"As a precaution, she created a powerful artefact, the Hand of Miera, an object with ultimate power over the Manastream. Enough to protect us should anything go awry. Naturally, something so powerful cannot be just left lying around where anyone can get it, but *you* could…"

"We'll do it!" Tharin burst out, he didn't need to know any more; he was raring to go.

"You don't even know what *it* is!"

"If it cures the sickness, does it matter?"

"Well, I guess not," Reyla admitted, her shoulders dropping. "But aren't we already on a quest to stop the witches?"

The spirit chuckled at them with that condescending tone Reyla found her elders usually do when they knew something she didn't. "Well, actually, you can do both at once.

"To reach the Hand of Miera, you must first travel to the shrines of the other nine ancestors and gain their blessing. It is likely the witches are using these shrines in other kingdoms to gain access to the Manastream. There, you must prove yourself and receive the blessing of the spirit within," Auldafrey explained simply. "Once you have received the blessing of all ten ancestors and proven yourselves worthy to wield the Hand of Miera, only then will we show you how to open the way to our Mother's temple.

"Take these, wear them always," he added, activating his artes as he waved his hands in their direction.

Two rings appeared, floating before Reyla and Tharin. They grabbed the rings, placing them over their finger - Reyla her left middle and Tharin his right index.

"These rings will serve as proof of your journey and will guide your way to the next shrine."

The metal warmed and warped as it slipped over Reyla's knuckles, shrinking to fit tight against her skin. It looked like a simple silver band with a single twist, but its mere presence reacted to the mana already stored within her body. An invisible beam breezed through her core like a warm gust of wind. Static ran to her fingertips as mana surged and rushed through her core.

"Okay, so ten shrines, ten spirits," started Reyla admiring the silver against her olivine skin.

"Ten blessings. What's a blessing do anyway?" asked Tharin.

"Each will be different. My blessing allows you the ability to heal as your ancestors once did," replied the spirit.

Reyla studied her palm, concentrating as she willed mana into her hand. Normally it would take half a minute to build up the required energy to activate her artes, but her palm went cold and glowed white within a few seconds. She closed her fingers, doubting even the Gods would be able to enhance her terrible proficiency with healing artes.

"Now, head south to Pudron where you will face your first trial," Auldafrey instructed, still hovering above them. "I wish you good luck. Once you reach the borders, you will be beyond my sights, and the world outside is in great turmoil.

"Be careful young Frey. Our hopes rest with you."

* * *

CHAPTER EIGHT

Elsafrey was startled awake when there was a knock at her office door.

"Enter," she called, brushing the sleep from her eyes.

Reyla and Tharin rushed in, their clothes dirty, their faces aghast.

"Your Grace." Reyla bowed. "We have news."

"You won't believe it," burst out Tharin, ignoring all formalities. "It's about the sickness."

Elsafrey held her response as the pair informed her of all that had transpired in the shrine below. Her stomach rolled to hear the sickness spread through the Manastream, her thoughts turning to her people who so actively used their artes.

She listened intently, her mind racing as she tried to piece together all the information. By the time they finished, she was troubled, but she remained silent and still as she decided how to proceed.

"This is distressing news…" She sighed. "And he says there's no other way to reverse it? Very well…"

Elsafrey went quiet and pressed her hands together as she mulled it over once more.

Could she allow them to go alone? A small party would have no problems accessing the shrine of Pudron, but other kingdoms were another matter entirely. As their numbers grew so would their profile, so perhaps it would be better to stay inconspicuous as just two. Although, that brought its own issues.

"This cloaked figure has me concerned," Elsafrey continued, her voice soft, but flowing quickly. "It stands to reason the intruder knew something was there, but without knowing their motives I think it best they continue to think we have not found the shrine ourselves."

The two guards gave quick nods.

"I think the best course of action is for us to take Auldafrey at his word, and move on the assumption that these witches are not friendly." Elsafrey paused, swallowing her emotions, taking in her gallant young soldiers proudly as she realised the magnitude of the task set before them.

"Take what you need from the depot," she ordered. "You will face the Trial of the Ten Ancestors and collect the Hand of Miera. Head south to Pudron and scout this first trial. I shall prepare for your return.

"Leave tonight.

"And do not tell anyone."

* * *

And so, on that dry summer night, two Frey raided the depot, where they packed bedrolls and filled packs with food and camping supplies. They exchanged their Queen's Guard uniforms for lighter leaf-leather armour and green travelling cloaks, attaching their shields to their packs and securing their sheathed swords to their belts.

In silence, they collected their packs and walked through the slumbering forest paths leading from Ceynas, the Life Tree guiding their way through the darkness. They passed by the twin stone bears of the cemetery gates, continuing south to where the glow of the Life Tree faded, marking the southern path of the Freya Road and the start of their journey.

The two wavered, staring intently at the natural boundary before them.

"You ready?" asked Tharin, turning to Reyla, excitement twinkling in his perennial-blue eyes.

"Yeah. Should we do this thing?" asked Reyla, starting their ritual.

"Yeah," grinned Tharin. "Let's."

* * *

FORGED IN FLAMES

13 MONTHS BMF

* * *

I'll admit I was happy.
Auldafrey chose his champions well.
Their plan could very well succeed.
I could only hope and pray Elsa and Ara could hold their
Kingdom together in the meantime.
However, there was still The Empire to consider…

* * *

CHAPTER ONE

High Priestess Elsafrey crossed to her bedside, her hair plaited and resting down the back of her nightgown. She removed her crown and placed it on the side before climbing under the duvet, ready for bed.

"We need to do something. I'm reaching my limits," she confessed to Galafrey as he washed his face. "I've searched every reference I can think of. All my research has done is confirm the warning from Auldafrey."

Galafrey dabbed his face dry. "Have you asked my mother?"

"We're not *that* desperate." She smirked. His mother was a hateful woman. "Come on, Gal, I'm serious. We cannot keep this to ourselves any longer. Our people are in pain. They need answers."

"And what do you propose we tell them?"

"That this sickness spreads through the Manastream. That everyone is susceptible," she replied firmly. "We need to consider prohibiting artes across the kingdom."

Galafrey withheld his concerns, folding his towel and hanging it over the back of a chair.

"The amount of mana we absorb naturally from the

Manastream is negligible," Elsafrey pressed. "If we abstain from using our artes and depleting our reserves, we will be less likely to develop the sickness."

"But not guaranteed. You cannot expect the whole kingdom to suddenly stop using their artes on the chance they will not get sick," Galafrey's monotone voice was tinged with disdain. "We rely on artes for agriculture, medicine, construction, to name but a few. The kingdom would fall to ruin within a matter of months."

"Then we should learn to adapt," she returned, her tone matching his as the tension grew between them. "We can teach our medics practical healing solutions. In Pudra they cauterize their wounds, and the Sudra pack them with sand. Other kingdoms yield crops without our artes, and build houses from stone."

"You know it's not that simple." Galafrey sighed as he extinguished the candles and crossed to his bedside. He removed his crown, joining her under the duvet.

"What do you propose we do in the meantime?" asked Elsafrey, unwilling to sleep until the matter was resolved. "We cannot merely sit and await the result of Godly quests when our people suffer."

"They always suffer. Our priority should be to the kingdom."

"It should be to the people," she snapped. The old ways were still deeply ingrained in many Frey - her husband included. "We cannot expect our citizens to place themselves in jeopardy for the sake of a greater harvest."

Galafrey paused, swallowing as he considered her

words. "Fine, I'll have Valren send an announcement out in the morning, but don't expect we will be able to enforce such an order."

Elsafrey smiled through her worry, and accepted the small victory. If they could just slow the spread of the sickness, it would give her time to find a treatment for their symptoms.

"We shall just have to hope our people make the right decision."

* * *

The forests were already awake as Arafrey crossed to the temple that morning, determined to find Reyla.

Today was the day. Arafrey had given Reyla enough space to sort through her feelings. It was time they talked. She just had to find Reyla first.

Arafrey's first disappointment came as she reached the temple to find Mika and Gurrien stationed by the entrance. She knew them from the Queen's Guard and the stories Reyla had shared, but she brushed past them without acknowledgement.

She entered the temple with Nasir in tow, stationing him by the entrance as she peered down the temple corridors. No guards were stationed down the east wing but two remained by the door to the catacombs. Arafrey didn't recognise them, nor did she care; neither were Reyla.

Disheartened, Arafrey turned to her duties. It

wouldn't be too hard to find an excuse to stay past the guard change during a pandemic. That was when she would catch Reyla.

"Good, I'm glad you're here." Elsafrey greeted her as she exited the courtyard. "Come, in here."

Elsafrey led her into the ward with the comatose patients. Here, the temple staff gathered between the beds, each dressed in cream robes and habits, their faces concerned.

"All present," said Sister Alma as she finished counting their heads.

"Good, then we may begin," replied Elsafrey, crossing to stand by the outer wall, her face like stone.

Arafrey tensed. She had no idea what was happening - she had only arrived at the temple early in hopes of finding Reyla on duty.

Elsafrey cleared her throat. "This morning, a kingdom-wide alert was issued by the crown. It reads as follows." She unrolled a notice she pulled from her robes. "The sickness which crosses our lands is caused by corrupted mana residing within our bodies. Use of artes exacerbates the condition and those using their artes are more susceptible. Therefore, we request all Frey to use discretion and only activate their artes under the direst of circumstances. Be vigilant and together we can make it through this crisis."

Arafrey continued observing as the sisters asked their questions. She held no doubt her mother would find a cure eventually. It was better all-round if she just stayed out of the way until then. Not that she had anything to do with Reyla absent. Visiting the twins was hardly a favourable option.

"With this ban in effect, we will need to refresh some of our practical healing skills," Elsafrey announced. "We have tomes on dressings and sutures, as well as detailed accounts of procedures..."

Arafrey couldn't maintain her concentration as Elsafrey spoke. All she could think about was Reyla.

If Reyla wasn't on duty in the temple, then perhaps she was patrolling somewhere. Tharin was also missing from her mother's usual staff, so it was possible they were stationed together.

Arafrey's fury bubbled to think that Reyla was going to such lengths to avoid her. They had known going in their relationship had an expiration date, but Reyla always had one ear to the wind - afraid they would be found out. It was one thing to struggle with their religion - many Frey considered same-sex relations an affront to nature - but to walk away over reputation was another thing altogether.

Arafrey's shoulders dropped as she sighed internally.

Part of her wished they were caught in the act and her reputation sullied. At least then she would have good reason to relinquish her title. She would prefer that to living the rest of her life preaching words she didn't believe.

"If you have any questions see Sister Alma. Do your best, ladies," finished Elsafrey, bowing her head to let them know she was done. "Ara, a moment."

Arafrey hung back as the sisters bowed and left the ward to tend their duties.

"With the courtyard occupied I will be moving sermons to the Pavilion for the time being, I need you to manage the temple while I'm away," said Elsafrey. "With this sickness thriving, we cannot afford to leave our patients unattended."

Arafrey was quick to agree. Any chance to avoid sermons was good with her. "Things seem to have quietened down a bit. Are you sure we still need so many guards in the temple? It feels like a war zone in here."

"We need the additional support with so many bodies in the temple. Patients keep wandering and I'd rather they not end up in the catacombs or medicine cabinet," her mother insisted, although it was a fair point Arafrey couldn't refute.

"Do you have any plans to replenish my staff?" Arafrey tried, planning to turn the conversation in her favour. "Nasir has been working double shifts all week."

"Captain Valren assures me you will have replacements by the end of the week. I'm sure they will do you well."

"Does that mean Reyla won't be coming back to my staff?" she asked, catching her tone so as not to rouse suspicion. "We had plans to go hiking for her birthday."

"She's been reassigned. Besides, Reyla's birthday is in Spring."

"Oh." Arafrey hesitated, she should have known her mother would know that.

Elsafrey sighed. "I know you two are close, but Reyla has a job to do. One she is quite capable of I'll add too. Don't worry, dear. I'm sure she'll come to visit you when she gets the chance."

Arafrey mumbled a weak agreement and returned to her duties. Whatever was going on, her mother wasn't going to tell her. One thing was for sure; Reyla was at the heart of it.

* * *

CHAPTER TWO

Nymati lay staring at the hieroglyphics painted on to her bedroom ceiling. Spans of black squared and squiggled over the sandstone, stretching and warping as her eyes unfocused. The symbols were supposedly there to promote strength and fertility within those who slept below them, their true meaning lost to many.

She closed her eyes, a blink that failed to make the return, her eyelids too heavy to raise. *How long had it been since she last slept?*

She was weak. The cramps in her stomach suggested it had been days since she last ate, but she had long given up. Food only turned to ash in her mouth.

How long since she last fed? She was so lost, lethargic. She wasn't sure she had the strength to do so, the thought bringing her only more pain.

Nymati turned, her ruby eyes opening to gaze at the space Drazah once filled. Her heart lurched to see he was not there. This was their bed, their room. It was wrong for him not to be there. So seldom did they leave each other's company, it was as if she functioned without a limb.

Their bedroom held so many fond memories for Nymati. Malaki had been born in the bed where she lay, likely conceived in there too. On mornings long ago the four of them would gather before breakfast, the boys all excited for one thing or another. And whenever there were fireworks, they would watch them from the balcony; the same balcony Drazah banished her to whenever he caught her smoking.

This room had been her sanctuary for so long, she wasn't sure where else to go. She was certain there was nowhere else she would rather be. Although, a small part of her was almost glad to be leaving it behind - the memory of her beloved Drazah too much to bear.

Her eyes moved to Drazah's desk, a wide polished birch monstrosity which dominated the corner of their bedroom. There was an office on the ground floor, but he had moved there to be closer to Nymati when she had been bedridden and pregnant. However, his chair remained empty, and his papers had been replaced with a ceremonial headdress, the gold and gems dull in the darkness.

Nymati's ribs pinched her aching heart, forcing her eyes closed once more.

The headdress sat in preparation for the emperor's arrival. His convoy had been spotted over the horizon that evening and was likely to reach them by noon.

The day Nymati dreaded was upon her.

Today she would don the ceremonial robes of her foremothers and do her final duty for her people. Today she would relinquish her title as queen and give her kingdom to the Empire.

This final act was all that kept Nymati going these last few weeks, her body and soul so broken she was ready for it all to end. If she could do nothing else, she promised herself she would complete the terms of her paramour's duel.

The thought near finished her. Her weak heart flailed as the last of her strength slipped through her fingers. Ready to give up, she curled in on herself, praying to the Gods for strength.

In Nymati's eyes, she didn't have two children, she had millions. The idea she would soon give them to someone such as the emperor struck her as hard as the loss of Drazah.

A growl swept through Nymati's body, bringing her brows to a sharp point. The thought of failure slicked her tongue with iron. *No, she would not allow it to end like this.*

Nymati threw back her bedsheet, reaching for her dressing gown. She wrapped the thin layer around her slender form as she headed for the bedroom door, entering the dimly lit corridors with dramatic flair.

Her dressing gown swept down the sandstone steps as she descended to the throne hall, crossing the grand sandstone floor with a grim ire. The aisle torches of the columns were still lit, creating a spotlight on the throne. Nymati averted her eyes, fixing them instead upon the stairs leading down into the sub-level of the palace.

A stern air surrounded Nymati as she continued into the temple below.

Built into the plateau of the palace, the temple was a

windowless shrine above all of Sudra. Torches and candles licked the temple walls with an orange glow, warming the Sudran Queen as she glossed past painted murals depicting Sudran history. All this led to the front of the temple where the golden statue of Asphet-Kau, first of the Sudra loomed over the benches. He held a golden sword in his hands, a relic dating back to the First Ones, which they used for ceremonies.

Although the temple was in honour of Asphet-Kau, it was the statue of Anneke-Sun, patron saint of female warriors, where Nymati knelt. From the floor, the hieroglyphics behind made it seem like she had radiant teardrop wings, her golden face strong and proud. She held an ornate staff in one hand, although this was merely a replica of the original, the pole reaching her knees as she set on the offensive. Nymati's gaze dropped to the feet of the statue, her eyes resting on a plaque, inscribed upon it the immortal words: "We Shall Endure".

She sighed. As a child of the wastelands, Nymati had no choice but to live her life by that saying. Sitting before the words usually brought her strength, but it seemed neither Nymati nor the statue had any more to give. She had endured all she could handle, pushed to the edge of her limits. She was certain any more would be the death of her.

"I failed you," she uttered, her hand reaching instinctively for the ruby necklace upon her bosom.

Nymati had come to seek guidance, but now she was there, her words and intentions became as lost as her.

"How can I…? This… This is all my fault…"

Nymati brushed away tears as footsteps descended the temple stairs. A young guard, marked out by his smock and sword, entered the temple. He started as he saw her.

"Your Grace, apologies. I didn't expect anyone to be down here so late," he said, bowing his head.

"I was just leaving," Nymati told him, although now she was faced with the prospect of returning to her empty bedroom, she wasn't sure why. "It is rather late…"

"Yeah, well I like to speak my prayers when they're important. Y'know, really make sure the Gods are listening." He grinned. "I get funny looks if I do it during the day."

"You know, perhaps in this room, they just might be listening," mused Nymati with a soft smile.

"I'd be honoured if you'd join me, Your Majesty," he offered, holding an arm out to the space before Asphet-Kau.

Nymati turned to the golden statue with wide eyes. Normally, she would politely decline such an invitation, but when faced with the alternative she decided to stay.

She joined the guard as he knelt, holding his hands together. Somehow prayer didn't feel like enough, but still, Nymati bowed her head and closed her eyes as the guard began.

"Lord Asphet, we thank you for the strength you give us to continue in these difficult times. We pray that you lend us your power and courage so that we may face The Empire…"

Nymati tuned out his words. She never felt the need to pray for strength or courage - those things she held in abundance. She had vanquished many foes in her time, becoming a legend among men. There was no challenge beyond her. Yet still, she was destined to fail. No matter how hard she prayed, how hard she worked, what happened now was beyond her control. She was as powerless as the man kneeling beside her.

By the same time tomorrow, it would be official.

Her stomach rolled.

"We give thanks to King Drazah. May he rest in peace with the knowledge he did his kingdom proud…"

Now there was a joke.

It was all Nymati could do to hold her snort in a sneer, for she believed Drazah's sacrifice to have been in vain. After all, what did Drazah's death achieve? They were still defeated. She was still to abdicate.

Soon, all would know of their impotence and there was nothing she could do about it.

Would it have been so bad to bend the knee? To watch as the emperor marched her people into a campaign of vanity and greed. Sitting silently by as her people were thrown into disgrace. It seemed she was destined to do so anyway. At least then Drazah would have been there to watch their demise with her.

But then what of their secret?

"May we rise to the challenge of tomorrow and learn from the failings of our past," continued the young guard, bringing his prayer to a close. "In the name of our forefathers, we shall endure, for the sake of our kingdom we survive."

Nymati lost her train of thought, smirking at the incorrect rendition of her peoples' sacred vows. However, her heart stopped, his words resonating within her, guiding her to the answers she so desperately sought.

She came to the Gods for answers, and they provided. Of course they wouldn't forsake her now. This was merely another test. She was Nymati Tamun, Emissary of the Desert, Demon Queen of Sudra, there was no challenge beyond her. She was a survivor. A fighter. A winner.

To think she was so close to giving up, to leaving her people. How could she? She had come so far, gotten so close, to give up now would be inconceivable.

Nymati's nostrils flared as she rose to her feet. A smile cracked over her cheeks as she thanked the guard, a devilish idea tickling her fancy. Her tongue traced the sharpened points of her fangs.

No… Her job wasn't over. Her people still needed her. Queen or not, her people still had a secret to protect. This was not the time to yield.

For the sake of her kingdom, she would survive.

* * *

Nymati waited before the double golden throne of Sudra. Alone.

A second raised platform reached out before her,

stopping by the ankles of those crowded into the hall. It was within this ten-metre square that the legend of Nymati began, the two decades between both too long and too short at the same time. She thought it only fitting her time as queen would end here also, although she hoped her legend would not fall into obscurity as with those who came before her.

Draped in white robes, Nymati held as still as the air around her, expressionless. The ceremonial headdress she had worn proudly so many times before seemed to grow in weight with every second she watched over her people, taking them in as if it would be the last time.

Citizens started arriving before breakfast. The throne hall quickly filled with various dignitaries and men of import from within Sudra, each dressed in their best formal wears - although for many that wasn't saying much. Even now her people filed into the streets below, gathering en masse to see their fallen king returned.

A part of Nymati was proud to see such a turnout, but pride soon turned to anguish as the throne hall doors swung open.

Sunlight poured in, the silhouette of the emperor blazed, black against a white canvas, and his shadow shot down the aisle like a spectre. Tensions rose bringing everyone to a stop, the spectators turning their heads in unison as the emperor marched towards Nymati.

He strode down the columned aisle with just enough confidence to remain humble yet imposing, a parade of soldiers behind him. The Sudra watched in furious silence, averting their gaze as the emperor passed, but Nymati held true, her eyes scanning over the emperor's hulking physique to rest on his face.

Dura typically had peachy complexions and round ears, but the emperor was far more tan, perhaps from his time spent on the battlefield. He was surprisingly well-groomed considering the journey he'd just had, his brown hair trimmed short, coming down into sideburns that led into a dark stubble across his cheeks and square jaw.

Nymati's attention caught on the emperor's eyes. Even at a distance, they burned ultraviolet; a curious trait even among the Sudra and not one she remembered him having.

They had met once, many years ago, when the emperor was still a boy and she just wed. Back then, there was nothing spectacular about him. He was even kind of weedy, but now… If he hadn't just invaded her kingdom and killed her king, she may have been impressed by the way he turned out.

The emperor's presence towered over the congregation as he stepped on to the platform and stopped before the throne. Nymati raised her chin to meet him, her facade never faltering. However, her heart failed her as she noticed the sleek wooden chest his Duran entourage left so unceremoniously in the aisle, on the floor, behind him.

It was as if her parabond shattered all over again. A lump grew in the back of her throat that held her breath. Her stomach churned, her eyes ready to burst as she realised what – or rather *who* - was in the chest.

At that moment there was no noise, no one else. Time at a standstill, Nymati stared unblinking at the flimsy wooden casket holding her beloved king.

Was he always so small?

"...My Lady."

Nymati turned as she realised the emperor was speaking to her.

"Welcome to our home," she managed, summoning what strength remained to give the emperor a deep curtsey.

Grand Master Barrick came forward to join them by the throne, a golden sword held across both palms as he shuffled over with incredible difficulty. He was an ancient Sudran who started to curl into himself as the years went on. His arms trembled as he offered the sword to Nymati.

"Thank you."

Nymati received the sword with gloved hands, the lace fabric a gesture of goodwill on her part. She adjusted her grip until it was firm and considered for a moment the possibility that she could succeed where her king could not.

She eyed the emperor, a predatory purr rippling her senses.

He would be unlikely to see it coming if she were to take the sword and swing. It wouldn't require much effort on her part, and the men he brought with him would be helpless in a room full of Sudra. The only question would be whether he was fast enough to stop her.

Knowing that the emperor bested Drazah both added to her temptation and stopped it at the same time. Despite the dais she stood upon, the emperor held head and shoulders above her. Even if that weren't the case, she doubted the sword possessed the strength to penetrate that thick neck of his: it was for ceremonies and wasn't especially sharp. Perhaps it was worth the risk, even if it meant her life, but what would become of her people if she perished?

With a heavy heart, the Sudran Queen drew a deep breath, preparing to perform her final official act for her people.

"I, Nymati Tamun, Emissary of the Desert and Queen of Sudra, do hereby surrender my kingdom along with all its property and holdings to you, Callius Gabris, King of Dura and Emperor of the Duran Empire," she proclaimed, filling the hall as she took the sword by the blade and offered the handle to the emperor.

The emperor received the sword, its handle so tiny in his giant palm, turning to the hall as he held it above his head. There were a few cheers from the Empire soldiers, accompanied by half-hearted claps from others, but there was no applause from the Sudra – only silence.

The silence stretched seconds into hours as the Sudra held still, leaving Nymati with a decision to make.

She could do nothing, watch as the silence turned into whispers and allow the seeds of discontent to spread among her people, leading to revolt and unrest. It was unlikely the emperor would be able to control her people, his attempts would fail, the following chaos serving as a distraction while Nymati worked from the shadows. Although, her people were already in a weakened position, would they be able to survive rebellion long enough for her to reclaim power?

Nymati tightened her jaw. She had never been so unsure as she stepped forward. Her thoughts on the oaths she once swore to protect her people, she faced the hall once more.

"My children, this is not a day for sadness." Nymati wet her lips in a futile attempt to combat sand in her throat. "Today is a day for you to prove yourselves.

"Our kingdom has faced many hardships, and it is how we face change which defines us as a people," Nymati projected, her ruby eyes scanning the congregation before her.

"Our king gave his life so that you may not have to. Do not let his sacrifice be in vain." Nymati's voice remained smooth, building into a cheer, her gloved hands warm as she held them out to her people.

"So hear me when I say, welcome change. Welcome the Empire. In the name of the fallen we fight. For the sake of our future, we shall endure!

"Show them all we are Sudra. And we're not going anywhere!"

The crowd erupted into applause as Nymati stood back to admire her handiwork, her fingers reaching habitually for her ruby necklace.

'Your sacrifice will not be in vain,' she promised the casket on the floor, still unable to bring herself to look toward it. *'I'll protect our people for both of us.*

'No matter the cost.'

Emperor Gabris sat upon the golden throne of Sudra, the double-width surprisingly comfortable as he watched the congregation crowd around Nymati. Her fragrance still lingered in the air around him, sweet like the honeysuckle back home.

Callius was impressed with Nymati, to say the least. Her rousing speech changed the atmosphere of the room completely, some Sudra were even smiling at him as they queued to see her. He smirked as Nymati met each citizen in turn, amused by the affectionate display from the supposed Demon Queen.

Nymati was a few years his senior but hadn't seemed to age in the time since they had first met. Her dark skin held no wrinkles and her hair remained jet black, when Callius himself had more than his fair share of wandering greys. Despite her burdens, Nymati still greeted each of her citizens with a genuine smile, the shine of her pearly fangs matched only by her golden jewellery.

Combined with her white robes, Nymati seemed almost angelic. It was easy to forget all she threatened. Perhaps the Sudra weren't the hardened warriors they claimed to be, although the many stories that came to mind had nothing to do with their skills in battle.

Callius shifted his weight. He doubted things would have ended so favourably if Nymati had been the one to head negotiations. He knew of no defence against Sudran artes and he heard Nymati could drain a man dry from twenty feet. She was truly a formidable opponent. One he could not afford to underestimate.

As the crowds dwindled, Nymati left her people and approached him, a young Sudran woman with silver hair by her side.

"Your Eminence," said Nymati as the two dipped into a bow. "This is Aeryn, my most trusted aide."

Nymati placed her hand over Aeryn's shoulder, the pair sharing a moment of intimacy as Aeryn smiled her thanks.

"She can take you anywhere you need to go and get anything you wish," said Nymati, prompting Aeryn to bow her head in agreement.

"I arranged a banquet for this evening and your chambers are ready for you when you need them," Nymati continued, the timbre of her voice seeming to lessen with every syllable. "I also made arrangements for all the women of our staff to wear gloves; I hope this puts your men at ease."

The emperor's eyes flashed to Aeryn, running over her smock to cotton gloves. He noted Nymati had on a pair herself, made from much finer white lace. He supposed the cotton ones would become rather uncomfortable in the current climate, but wondered if lace would be enough to save him from Sudran Charm.

"Please, let me know if you have any issues," said Nymati plainly.

Her demeanour gave Callius pause. The memory of their first encounter had left an impression which remained with him for twenty years. However, looking at her now, Nymati seemed less omnipotent than before, broken even. Her eyes never met his, and the charisma he so vividly remembered was just... *gone*.

"I would like to have a look around the palace, I've not been since I was a lad. It's much smaller than I remember," he said looking around the hall. "Would you like to join me?"

He caught Nymati struggle, panic flashing behind the ruby of her eyes before asking; "Is that an order, Eminence?"

The question caught him off guard. Did he say something wrong? Her voice was weak, pathetic, not at all like the woman who stood before the crowds moments before. Certainly not the woman he dreamed of once again seeing after all these years.

"No, no of course not."

"It's just, I would like to bury the-" Nymati caught herself. "-My husband."

"Oh! Yes, of course," Callius stumbled, embarrassed he hadn't thought of that sooner. "Please, as you will."

Nymati bowed and hurried away, leaving him alone with Aeryn.

"Please, follow me, Sire," offered Aeryn, her voice barbed with contempt. Her eyes never left him, a quiet storm brewing within her stony stare which urged him to caution.

Despite his cold welcoming, Callius found himself giddy as Aeryn led him through the palace. He fell into exploration like a child, insisting she explain what each of the rooms were used for, and answer his many follow-up questions.

The palace was built upon a large stone plateau overlooking the city, its history dating back to the First Ones. Its ground level held the main throne hall and dining room, as well as some administrative rooms and the kitchen.

"This room served as the previous king's office," said Aeryn as she opened the door to an empty, unused room. She may have caught his surprise as she added, "This office gets no air, so Drazah preferred to work elsewhere."

Aeryn then led him up a flight of stairs, coming out on a roof terrace filled with flower beds containing vegetables. They returned indoors, inspecting the library and display rooms, although neither were much when compared to his own.

"The rest of this floor is storage and bedrooms," Aeryn told him as they wandered down the sandstone corridors. "Currently only Nymati and her sons are in residence. We had the rest cleared for your arrival."

Callius managed a response, but his eyes watched the doors they passed, and a stray thought wondered which room Nymati now resided in.

He followed Aeryn up another flight of stairs until reaching a double door on the top floor. She pushed the doors open to reveal a large suite with a small balcony overlooking the rest of the palace.

Callius' attention was instantly drawn to the ceiling.

Dark hieroglyphics decorated the tops of every wall within the palace, black and purple motifs that seemed to repeat every ten feet or so. However, in the suite the pattern expanded over the ceiling, creating a work of art both beautiful and haunting to look at. If he squinted, Callius could make out the shapes of objects and perhaps even a face or two. A shiver ran down his spine.

"Her Highness had us ready the room for your arrival," came a voice. Callius startled having forgotten Aeryn was still with him.

He cleared his throat. "Very well. You may leave," he told her. Already he knew he didn't like Aeryn, but so far, she had given him little cause to complain. "I shall be down for the feast."

Aeryn gave a low bow before leaving without a word.

Now alone, Callius crossed the muggy room to the balcony.

Outside there was no breeze, only more hot, dry air. The sun beamed down through a cloudless sky - not even the Manastream interrupted the clear view as he admired the city that was now his.

The city of Halda seemed to go on for miles; row after row of sun-bleached shacks reaching off into the horizon. The river Ballish cut through the middle, regularly stretching to over a mile in width as it continued south to provide water and a much-needed dash of colour to an otherwise cruel landscape. Despite merging with the river Leste, the Ballish was narrower in the city and this narrowing allowed for bridges in strategically placed points throughout the city.

To the east, the Sudran funeral procession reached the outskirts. They crossed the sands towards what he thought of as the cemetery, the sacred grounds marked by large sandstone statues still visible even at a distance.

Thousands of Sudra still crowded in the tatty streets, the masses held together in solemn solidarity behind their former king and queen.

Callius leant upon the solid parapet.

The people of Sudra were poor, that much was true, but they were worth far more than the lands and treasures he had obtained. In just a few short hours he had seen the Sudra display strength of character and loyalty far greater than any Duran. Perhaps, if he could return them to their former glory, the Sudra would follow him as they did Nymati.

Callius mentally listed all the changes he wished to implement as they toured the palace. The thought of all the work he had to do coursed through his veins as he admired the view, a crooked smile breaking across his face.

Finally, a challenge worthy of him.

* * *

Amynus waited for his mother and Master Barrick to descend into the royal crypt before making his escape.

He weaved through the crowds, his head down in a bid to return to the palace unnoticed. Best to leave the proceedings before his mother could demand he attend the banquet that evening. The stone boundaries of the burial grounds were almost in sight when a heavy hand clapped against his shoulder.

"Amynus," came a familiar deep voice.

Amynus turned, greeting Sabutok warmly. As Captain of the Palace Guard, he ran the Sudran Army's barracks, at least for the time being. A trusted member of his father's inner circle, Sabutok's bald head was a familiar sight at family events.

"How you doing, kiddo?" he asked, flashing oversized fangs in a wide smile. "Me and the lads are off to the Sandwyrm, you're welcome to join us."

"Yeah, sounds good. I could do with the distraction."

"And then some, you look like you've aged a decade," teased Sabutok, the scar over his forehead creasing as he wiggled his brow. "Come on, I'll walk with you."

"Honestly, these last few weeks have been rough," Amynus admitted, sand collecting in his sandals as they returned to the city proper. "Until this morning we thought I'd be the one performing the ceremony today."

"That bad huh?"

"Yeah. Mother looked like death when I saw her yesterday," Amynus replied, his voice dipping as they entered the city streets. "I guess Aeryn must've force-fed her after I left."

"Have a little faith, your mother's among the best of us," Sabutok assured. "You're too young to remember what it was like before your grandparents retired, but your parents've done a lot for our people."

"So I hear," Amynus huffed, well aware of the footsteps he trailed. A part of him was glad he wasn't a prince anymore, the task of living up to his parents' legacy now falling to some other poor soul. Still, that didn't lessen the pain of losing his father any.

"Have you given any thoughts as to what you're doing next?" asked Sabutok, as they passed by the barracks, the training yards and sparring pits oddly silent. "You know you'll always be welcome in the barracks. You were planning on joining anyway, would it be the worst thing to slum it with the rest of us?"

"And serve under the bastard who killed my father?" Amynus barked, his mana surging with his tone.

"Look, I get you're angry, but a job's a job. Men like us aren't made to be scholars or artisans," Sabutok explained, his honesty bitter to swallow but true, nonetheless. "The boss may change, but the job's still the same. Besides, he'll likely leave half of us here to mind the palace while he goes back to Dura. At worst we're looking at a posting in Puwhar or something."

"I suppose."

"Just think about it. Who knows how long the Empire's gonna be in charge, no reason you should go hungry in the meantime is there?"

Amynus grinned in response as the Sandwyrm came into view, the plateau of the palace casting a cool shadow over the surrounding buildings.

"Now then, let's drink to that dumbass father of yours, and find ourselves a mighty great big pair of tits to bury our woes in," Sabutok declared, pushing open the bar doors.

"First round's on me!"

* * *

CHAPTER THREE

"Ugh! Are we there yet?" groaned Tharin, lifting his pack off his shoulders.

"Almost. Everham isn't far now," Reyla assured him, having quickly resumed her role as the responsible adult. "You've been to Pudron before, right?"

"Yeah, but we headed straight to Haston every time. I've not seen much more than the palace and that dingy bar Gurrein dragged us to."

Reyla chuckled, remembering the anecdote and the subsequent hangover well.

Having left the Freya capital, Ceynas, Reyla and Tharin followed the Freya road south as far as Asenya, a merchant town. From Asenya they traipsed the Nasai-ten south towards the Pudron border, passing by the Gretreen, a stone monument left in tribute to the Manastream.

The pair made good time, hitching lifts from merchants between the smaller villages, and passing into Pudron within two weeks. However, travelling and sleeping rough was already beginning to grow tiresome.

"Where d'you think the shrine is anyway?" asked Tharin.

"I'm not sure…" Reyla replied, trailing off as a gentle throbbing on her finger caught her attention. It wasn't a painful sensation - more warm than sharp - like static all around the ring on her finger. She wondered what it was.

"I swear, I think I'm allergic to this ring," moaned Tharin, holding his hand up for inspection. "It's making my skin all weird."

Reyla blinked, worried she had spoken her thoughts aloud.

"I feel it too. Maybe it's the rings showing us where the shrine is," she offered, the tingling sensation returning at the mere mention of shrines. "Perhaps we're just too far away to feel it properly."

"Hmmm," Tharin agreed, wiping his brow before returning his hands to the straps of his backpack.

Compared to Freya, Pudron was a warm, dull land. The Freya forests quickly dwindled into nothing, leaving behind yellowed fields and an uneven landscape, broken by lone trees and Pudran settlements in the distance.

Reyla thought it a nice change to see clear blue skies rather than thick foliage. The horizon stretched out beyond her sights in either direction, the sun warm as the mystic blue Manastream swirled around the atmosphere. Far to the south, the smoking peaks of five active volcanoes dominated Pudron's terrain where the Manastream converged. Reyla hoped the temple they sought would not be too far up them - but history had already proven her luck wasn't that good.

"You know, I still remember your first shift on the

Princess' Guard. Do you remember? We came down south to see the meteor shower," said Tharin as he looked to Reyla, taking stock of her quickly. "I was in total awe of you. I mean, you were a hero and had the battle wounds to prove it. I was so jealous."

"Really?" Reyla scoffed, entirely surprised. "I couldn't even hold my sword properly. I had to learn how to use my left hand just to get reinstated. I was just so sick of sitting around…"

"Well I couldn't tell," grinned Tharin. "And the princess certainly appreciated having you around."

Reyla just smiled as she always did when people made comments about the princess.

Of course Reyla remembered her first shift on the Princess' Guard. She was certain she could remember every moment she had spent with Arafrey if she allowed herself.

Her first shift, the Princess' Guard travelled south to stay in the Pudron palace in Haston, the capital. Arafrey had kept them up until the early hours of the morning to watch the meteor shower with Prince Logan. Although it was late, Arafrey had still called Reyla into her room before retiring.

Even back then, the princess had been skilled with healing artes, and had only allowed Reyla to come along on the proviso that she allowed Arafrey to tend her wounds. Reyla had received her promotion to the Princess' Guard after sustaining a near fatal sword wound during the war against Sheya, which had broken her collarbone and sliced down her back, narrowly missing her spine.

Although it had been months since her injury at the time, she still had a thick black scab that ran red around the edges where the skin scarred over.

Reyla had undressed her torso as instructed and waited quietly; the memory of holding her arms to her chest, embarrassed, still vivid years later. Her heart had pounded as Arafrey's hand touched her skin. Shivers called the hair on the back of her neck to attention, goose flesh covering her body as Arafrey ran her hands over the wound.

Reyla had struggled to hold still, her hand trembling as mana surged through her shoulder, cool but soothing. Her nerves and muscles rejoiced as they relaxed and her shoulder unwound.

"How's that feel?" Arafrey had asked as she ran her hand over Reyla's shoulder one last time.

"Much better, thank you."

Reyla had rushed for her clothes, regretting every inch of her body that was on show. She'd pulled on her tunic, turning to find Arafrey remained behind her.

"Princess?" Reyla had asked, her voice awash with concern.

"Um… Reyla…" Arafrey had mumbled, her emerald eyes to the ground as she assembled her words. "I know it's not proper, but do you think you could stay here with me tonight? It's just this room makes me rather uneasy."

"Of course, Princess," Reyla had replied without thought.

A quick look had told Reyla why Arafrey didn't like

the room; the Pudra were proud of their hunting trophies and arranged many around the palace. In particular, three wolf heads, their faces burdened with eternal fury, hung over the fireplace, directly across from Arafrey's bed.

Reyla had caught herself looking at them and shuddered. She didn't blame Arafrey for feeling uncomfortable. Besides, Reyla was more than happy to oblige. She got to avoid another hangover from Gurrien and that night fell asleep in an armchair, content and prideful, watching over her princess.

Reyla had woken the next morning to find that Arafrey had covered her with a sheet sometime during the night. She smiled, wondering when Arafrey had awoken, a strange warmth coming over her as she gathered herself and slipped away to join the rest of the guard.

The memory caused a goofy grin to warm Reyla's cheeks as she walked. Looking back, she realised that perhaps that was the moment she truly fell for her princess. A small act of compassion that bolstered their friendship and guided them towards something more.

Reyla cleared her throat and collected her thoughts. She took that memory, and any other feelings she still harboured for her dear princess, and banished them to the dark waters of her memory, along with the rest of her demons.

With a hopeless sigh, Reyla returned her attention to the road ahead and willed herself to keep moving forward. There was no looking back now.

'It's better this way,' she told herself.

'It's better for everyone…'

But that didn't stop it from hurting.

* * *

CHAPTER FOUR

Amynus spent much of his evening staring into a stein. Many were raised in honour of his father, the soldiers cheering as the higher-ups sang Drazah's many praises, yet still, his spirits remained low.

He held the stein with both hands, clicking his sharp nails against the rim. The image of the emperor holding their sacred sword still burned into his memory.

Amynus never imagined a Duran could grow so large. His surprise burst a sizeable hole in his quest for vengeance. He held no hopes of defeating such a colossus, the realisation significantly dampening his anger towards his father - and the unbridled anger turned instead towards his mother. A foul taste gurgled at the back of his throat as he thought of her addressing the crowds on the emperor's behalf.

Amynus sneered into his beer. He had seen the bloodlust in her eyes as she received the sword from Barrick. She'd had the emperor in her sights. He knew she had. So why didn't she swing?

"You'll get better answers from an elephant than the bottom of a beer mug," cooed a soft voice.

"Taldi?" He gasped, sitting back in disbelief to admire

the woman before him. "What're you doing here?"

"I came as soon as I heard," she replied, long white hair whisking on the stale air as she slipped into the chair across from him. "How're you doing?"

"Why does everyone keep asking me that?" He released his stein to the ale-soaked table between them.

"Because they care about you."

"Is that why you're here?" he asked without hesitation, his azure eyes on hers to gauge her reaction.

She looked away. Amynus rolled his eyes, doing the same in response.

The pair had once been close. He'd thought perhaps they'd marry someday, but his hopes had been swifty extinguished as Taldi was selected to join his mother's personal staff.

Among the Sudra, there were few honours so great. The girls chosen to serve under Nymati were trained to the highest standards, often leaving her employ for even greater heights. For orphans and vagabonds like Taldi, it was a dream come true - but it came at a cost.

"So, who'd she marry you off to? Or am I not allowed to know?" He rubbed a hand over his horns in some misguided attempt to comb his hair.

"It's not … you know I can't tell you."

"Did Mother send you? Did she bring you back just to spy on me again?" he accused her, the betrayal still raw.

"No, she can't know I'm here," warned Taldi, shaking her head.

"Then why? Why now?"

"Because I know you," she hissed, her voice dropping to a furious whisper. "I see the fire burning in your belly. I'm begging you. Please, Amynus, whatever you're planning on doing, don't do it."

"You have no right to ask that of me."

He had implored her not to serve under his mother, but the power Nymati had promised was worth far more than any affection Amynus had to offer. She had made her decision. Who was she to question his?

"Don't be so foolish. You know as well as I, you're no match for the emperor in your condition."

"In my condition?" Amynus exclaimed. It would have been less painful if she had just torn his heart out with her bare hands. "You come back after all these years as if nothing ever happened, and–"

"Please, Amynus," she begged, reaching across the table, taking his hand in hers. "Please, for old times' sake."

Old times' sake - meaning the many times she stormed into his bedroom, starved of mana, to feed on him. The first time taking his virginity.

The warmth of her charm engulfed his hand, sweeping along his arm and over his chest, as one by one, his senses relaxed. A soft smile crept towards his ears as he found himself remembering nights the two would spend together not so long ago. Their eyes met as she brushed her thumb over his.

It would be so easy for him to forgive her. He was so lost at that moment the familiarity would be most welcome. He was too proud to admit he had missed her all this time, but he couldn't deny it would be nice to have her around. Although, he would never be certain if it was Taldi or her charm he was so fond of.

"You're just as bad as she is." Amynus gritted his teeth, pulling his hand away. "You just don't get it, neither of you do."

"Amyn–"

"I'd better not see you around here again," he warned her, pushing on his mana enough to attract the attention of those around them.

"One day you'll see her as I do," he growled, slamming both hands on the table as he lifted to his feet. "I only pray for your sake, you don't burn all your bridges in the meantime."

And with that, he left.

* * *

Emperor Gabris sat back with a satisfied groan.

"I needed that," he declared to no one in particular, lifting his empty wine glass to notify one of the servers he wanted more.

As promised had Nymati arranged a banquet for him and his men. She was the perfect host, but remained quiet, staring off into the distance unless addressed directly.

The banquet was held in the throne hall, allowing him to lounge in his new throne as his men gathered around long tables to each side. His men grew merry, partaking in the feast greedily, even though it was lacking in quality compared to what they were used to.

A steady stream of performers filled the platform before him. Presently, a Sudran contortionist balanced upon a small stool as she touched her toe to her nose.

Callius sipped his wine, the bouquet hempy. They had finished eating a while ago, but they remained to finish the wine and watch the show. He relaxed into the throne, acutely aware of the storm brewing in the seat beside him.

If he was honest, Callius didn't blame Nymati for her foul mood. The circumstances of their reunion were far from ideal, and she had every right to hate him. However, he needed her support going forward if he didn't want to face an uprising from her people.

"You've outdone yourself, these performers are amazing," he offered, watching as a server replenished his drink. "Your people are marvellous."

Nymati agreed lazily, her eyes on the performers as she reached into her dress, bringing out a small silver tin. Almost instinctively, she opened the tin, pulling out a rolled cigarette. She placed the cigarette to her ebony lips and returned to the tin for a match. Still watching the performers, she struck the match against the tin, holding the flame against the paper as she inhaled.

Callius watched with curiosity. Smoking was an uncommon habit in Dura but very popular with the Pudra and Rugla. He supposed only those in good standing in Sudra would be able to afford such a novelty. Then again, Nymati was no ordinary woman.

A bolt of static hit Callius as Nymati's eyes flicked to catch his, noting his interest.

"Drazah didn't like me smoking. He said it was unbecoming of a queen." She depressed as she exhaled, an earthy smell falling over them as the smoke clouded in the non-existent breeze. "Guess I don't have that problem any more..."

Her tone was joking, she even gave a half-hearted chuckle, but the undertones were blue.

"I hear he confided in you often." Callius returned his eyes forward as three dancers graced the stage. "Your people seem to look up to you too. I'd appreciate your guidance going forward."

"My people are proud, and value honour above most anything else. Allowing me to bury their king will go a long way towards winning them over." Nymati's eyes fixed upon the performers as she spoke. Diligence straightened her back and duty weighted her words, as she casually drew on her cigarette between pauses. "I also have you to thank for that. Not everyone would have returned his body intact."

Callius flashed a smile as they returned to their awkward silence.

Conversation had never been so frustrating. No matter how he tried, everything circled back to the fact that he had killed her king and invaded her kingdom. Was it his fault Drazah challenged him? Was it his fault the Demon King underestimated him? Of course not. Yet it seemed Nymati had no intentions of moving on anytime soon.

"So how did you win over your people? They adore you." He was right, but flattery was always a good way to make people like you. Not that he was overly sure why he cared what Nymati thought of him - he was Emperor after all.

"Becoming queen was no easy task," she told him, her cigarette burning towards her gloved fingers as she held it before her luscious lips. "When I earned my place, I won their respect. Once I became queen I gained their love, which was even harder."

Nymati chose her words wisely, speaking with purpose and meaning - as any good queen should. Her voice was smooth yet commanding, every syllable calling him in like a sonnet.

Somehow, she made him feel weak and strong at the same time. Unsure yet determined, a warm chill ran down his spine as he dared himself to look upon her face.

"And how did you become queen?"

"When Drazah came of age, there was a tournament. It's a tradition of ours to ensure our bloodlines stay strong and our leaders prodigious," she replied, her voice unchanging. "It's a long story, but the short of it, after all was done, I had won. We married and later I became queen."

"And the long version?"

Nymati smiled and, for the first time, she held his gaze.

"I cheated," she said, a sinful smile cracking to the left as she stubbed out her cigarette.

Callius was clearly intrigued, but she didn't expand her story any further, which only made him want to know *so* much more.

* * *

CHAPTER FIVE

Reyla squinted hard at the door before them.

The door itself didn't bother her. She had already knocked and was waiting for someone to answer. It was what the door and the adjoining fifteen-foot fence represented which bothered her. Fencing in an entire town was certainly not a common practice among the Pudra, so why was it there?

They arrived outside Everham, a Pudran town a few days north of the volcanoes. It was much warmer this far south and the dry air hung thick with a constant burning smell.

A hatch about five feet up the door snapped open and a pair of bright yellow eyes in a red furry face leered at her.

"State your business," came a harsh voice.

"Passing through, we'd like to buy supplies."

"Two bronze." The eyes darted to Tharin. "Each."

Reyla fumbled through her pocket for change, passing it through the hatch. The door creaked open, and the two Frey received their first view of Everham.

It was a bustling town filled with square wooden buildings, the planks unevenly crafted and lacking the elegance of Frey architecture. The dirt road they followed ran through the middle of town. It was framed on either side by large glass-fronted shops below haggard signs with crudely spelt names.

The two Frey pressed on in search of a grocer, their noses high and breaths caught as they stepped over mounds of horse dung and drunkards littering their route. They scanned the shop fronts, finding tailors, fabulous glassware, blacksmiths, taverns and butchers, but nary a vegetable in sight.

While the Frey and Pudra were close allies, the Frey always looked down on their southern friends, Reyla included. In her experience, the Pudra were unclean, unmannered and, in most cases, drunk and screaming profanities for no apparent reason, which was entirely impolite and un-Frey-like.

Reyla likened them to weasels with their narrow faces, pointed ears and wet noses. They even had a handful of thick whiskers coming out of their cheeks and thin tails which often trailed down to their knees. Each grew the same brown or reddish fur with white markings over their fronts, although this was often discoloured by layers of ash, dirt and dust.

The two Frey criss-crossed the town in search of supplies, the streets filling as Pudra descended on the taverns. Reyla had all but given up hopes of finding supplies, when the scent of baked goods caught her nose. She followed it to a modest bakery.

Its window was much smaller than the other shops, with a sign no bigger than a handkerchief and a name invoking more thoughts of butter than bread. She may have missed it altogether if not for Tharin's interest in the two horses tied to a post outside, their tails swatting at flies as they waited patiently for their owners to return.

"Welcome, welcome," came an unseen voice as they entered. "Won't be a second."

The bakery boasted a few cabinets displaying a range of baked goods. A long counter ran across the middle of the shop, dividing it. The aroma of freshly baked bread was enough to return Reyla home to the palace, but an underlying smell of burning wafted in from a room beyond the counter.

A clattering of metal announced the shop keepers' arrival.

"Sorry about that," he started, mopping his furry brow with a rag. "Damn oven's got a mind of its own. What can I get you?"

They placed their order, and explained their situation.

"See, we don't get many Frey down this way," the Pudran explained as he accepted their coin. "There's a merchant two streets over who does fresh, but there's a premium on imports this far south."

Reyla watched her goods with intent, as the Pudran wrapped them in thin burlap, acutely aware of the merchant's sooty nails against her bread.

"Two streets which way?" she asked, receiving their purchase.

"East. You know, I think I have some Frey biscuits somewhere if you'd like?" the baker offered with a sharp toothy smile.

Reyla politely declined, unable to usher Tharin out the door fast enough, shuddering at the thought of Frey 'Somewhere' Biscuits.

* * *

It was early evening by the time they bought their supplies and found their way to the southern gate. However, a guard stopped their exit.

"'Fraid the gate's locked, you'll 'ave to wait 'til mornin'," the guard told them.

"I guess a bed wouldn't be the worst thing in the world," shrugged Tharin, counting the coin in his pocket.

Reyla agreed lazily, again cautious of the fence towering over them. At first, she thought it was designed to fleece travellers of their coin, but upon closer inspection, she wasn't so sure.

It appeared to be a recent construct, the soil holding the base was still damp in places and many of the beams lacked supports others boasted. Even compared to the unpolished designs of Pudran architecture, the wall seemed hastily constructed and unfinished, leaving Reyla uneasy.

'What were the Pudra so desperate to hide from?' she wondered, following Tharin back into Everham proper.

* * *

The two Frey ambled through the narrow side streets to a shabby four-storey building with 'Da In' crudely painted above the door. Here they booked a room, storing their kit before returning to the bar making up the ground floor for dinner.

The Da In was as shabby on the inside as it was on the out. The furnishings were misshapen and flimsy looking, and the walls were littered haphazardly with weapons, hats and hunting trophies, much to the disgust of the two Frey. Everything was shrouded in a thin layer of soot, making the room seem unnaturally dark, but it hummed with a warmth that radiated from the patrons as they danced around in inebriated bliss.

It was a far cry from the humble tavern they frequented back home – but it was homey as the Pudra welcomed the two Frey with open (*albeit possibly flea-ridden*) arms.

They perched on the edge of a table with a reasonably quiet group of Pudra. Tharin was in his element, instantly striking up a conversation as they ate their steamed vegetables and drank their beer.

The Pudra were dab hands at drinking and regaling their comrades with over-exaggerated tales of mischief-making and intrigue. Naturally, Reyla expected not even half of them to be true, although Tharin was not much better.

"We met the Agrana Prince back when I was on the Princess' Guard," he told the table. "His guards were near twice my size, but thick as The Life Tree!"

"I heard Sudra transformations are the size of elephants," added Nella, the Pudra to Tharin's left, her fur more orange than red. "All the best stories come from Sudra... You don't think they'll join The Empire do you?"

"Let's hope not," belted out Toya, sitting to Tharin's right, grey fur running through his temple suggesting he was older than he looked. "Estra and Puwhar are small potatoes compared to us *real* arte users. The Empire's got no chance against us otherwise."

"What d'you mean *'real arte users'*?" Tharin accused, sparking a heated debate over which arte was best.

Reyla made no comment, instead listening, laughing and pretending to be a part of the festivities.

She found herself seated beside a rather beastly Pudra. He was easy enough to ignore, making few attempts to join in their conversations, but she was very aware of his presence. His odour, in particular, gave her cause for concern, but she held her repulsion as he sat smiling to himself, saving his attention for the steady stream of beers delivered to the table.

"Don't let her quiet nature fool you," said Tharin, causing Reyla's eye to twitch as she returned to the conversation. "Our Reyla here's got more commendations than you've had beers."

"By Igniros, that's a mighty sum," cried Toya, slamming his stein on the table, causing all manner of drinks to spill their contents.

Although not overly religious, many of the Pudra prayed to the volcano god Igniros, however, these were mostly prayers for the volcano to not erupt this week or to send them some kind of good fortune. Some believed Igniros lived within the volcanoes and that the volcanoes would only erupt when they had done wrong, but these were in the minority and the vast majority of them were hapless heathens - according to the Ignorian scriptures anyway.

"It's not that many," Reyla insisted, her voice barely audible over the ruckus of the bar.

"Gah! Ignore her," Tharin scolded, waving her off. "I've got one story where she saves Galafrey, one with Arafrey and another where she took on the Guard Captain all by herself!"

Reyla sunk back into herself, allowing Tharin to retell exaggerated accounts of what he believed to be her accomplishments. Their Pudran companions revelled in Tharin's recital as he swung his arms about to enact her moments of reputed glory; not that he was witness to any of it...

* * *

A few too many drinks later, Tharin sat back. His cheeks warmed as his eyes lulled and a quiet came over him.

Reyla couldn't help but feel envious. A room filled with so many drunken, loud strangers was enough to ravage her senses. It was suffocating. Not that she would feel any better in a room filled with drunken people she knew, that was just who she was. Still, she couldn't help but feel like she was missing out as she observed the festivities - those around her ignorant of the turmoil plaguing her.

"So, what brings you down this way?" asked Toya, his demeanour a lot more subdued now it was just the two of them.

She did well to avoid direct conversation, but with Tharin enjoying his nap, she had no choice but to talk for herself. Thankfully the dwindling numbers did much to lessen her apprehensions.

"Scouting mission," she lied. The Pudra were nice enough, but she considered none of them trustworthy. "Her Majesty was hoping to visit some old temples of yours."

Reyla caught her reflexes as a hand fell to the bench beside her. The sensation of the warm paw against her leggings prickled the hair on the nape of her neck, sending a shiver through her senses. She held on to her features as her lip threatened to curl. Blood rushed to her extremities as she sized up the paw's owner more thoroughly, ready to act.

The disgusting Pudra hadn't moved all night. Swaying gently in the seat beside her, he only opened his mouth to put something in it, often missing and spilling his bounty down his grotesquely stained shirt instead. Having observed him consume ale like blueberries, it was a shock he was still conscious. Deciding quickly that the Pudra was oblivious to the intrusion on her personal space, Reyla turned back to Toya.

"If you're going up the 'cano best be careful," he warned. "There's some great ol' ruins up there. Though they were abandoned when the wyverns moved in."

Reyla remained focused on Toya as the Pudra beside her shuffled further along the bench. She resisted the urge to return his stare as he fixated on her, staring intently as his thumb brushed her thigh. *Was he testing her?*

"Is that why you built the fence?" she asked, gulping down a flurry of emotions with her beer as the paw reached over her thigh. She pushed it away without acknowledgement, the sensation of the sweaty palm lingering on her leggings churning her stomach.

"No, that's much more recent," Toya continued, unaware. "The animals 'round here started getting more aggressive, bigger even. Then they started getting brave and coming into the village at night. People started getting sick-"

"Your people are sick?" Reyla burst out, using the moment to push away the Pudra beside her, this time with more force. An evening in the bar was enough to show Reyla that the Pudra's idea of courtship was lacking compared to the more sophisticated Frey. Even so, she was getting frustrated and the beer in her belly warmed fast.

"Yeah, a fair number too," said Toya. "Got harder to protect everyone, like, so we built up the fence."

"When was this?"

"Maybe a few months ago now," Toya suggested, taking a swig of his drink as once again the hand returned to Reyla's thigh. "It's pretty dangerous out there -"

THWACK!

This time, Reyla grabbed the Pudran's wrist with her right hand, pulling it up on to the table. Simultaneously, she drew her knife with her left, hammering the blade into the table and splintering it between his fingers. Tharin snorted, jolting awake for the briefest moment before sinking back to sleep.

"Touch me again and I won't miss," Reyla hissed through clenched teeth, her eyes burning into his, unblinking.

The man recoiled off the bench, falling to the floor, but Reyla held firm, a combination of anxiety and resentment holding her still as she stared him down. Her fury relentless, Reyla watched as he collected himself from the floor and hurried away, but still, her heart skipped beats.

The fire still blazed behind her hazel eyes, her hand clenched tight around her knife, when Toya gave a loud satisfied chuckle.

"Although, now I think the wyverns may not be a problem..."

Reyla smirked. She'd trust a wyvern over a man any day.

* * *

Reyla nudged Tharin awake as Toya bid her farewell, hoisting him on to her shoulders as they struggled up the narrow staircase to their bedroom. Tharin had never been good at holding his alcohol, and he leaned on Reyla for support, standing only long enough to stagger across their small room before dropping face-first into the bed.

Reyla chose to leave him there, loosening the ties on her armour and undressing to her base layers. She placed her belongings neatly to the side, stretching out her arms behind her neck in hopes of releasing some of the tension. She rubbed the joint and up to her neck with her left hand, pressing deep into the muscle and along the dark scar.

Reyla had never been skilled in healing artes. She had some skills with plants and animals, but healing was more Arafrey's forte. However, since receiving the blessing from Auldafrey, Reyla had noticed a marked improvement in her abilities, and she practised each night before bed. She found that focusing her energy was much easier than the intense concentration she was accustomed – and that it built within her palm and activated her artes much faster than before she received their first blessing.

Frey healing artes used the mana stored within the body to create an external reaction to manipulate natural materials, their bodies included. The sensation was like placing her hand in ice, starting with her palm, spreading out to her fingertips. Her palm glowed soft white as the energy gathered, ready for the process to begin.

Reyla held her hand against the scar, wincing as the cool mana made contact with her tender shoulder. Her skin tingled as the mana soothed her aches and the pain slowly ebbed away. With old wounds such as hers there was little more she could do except dull the nerves, but it offered her the relief she required. She smiled, internally cheering at her success, and stretched out her arm, glad to be back to the dull ache she was sure would never fade.

Back home, Arafrey would soothe her shoulder often and Reyla had long become accustomed to the relief. As such, the lessened pain was bittersweet as she thought of her dear princess, and climbed into bed.

Reyla groaned as her head hit the pillow, instantly regretting the thought.

Sleep always eluded Reyla. Memories she had long tried to forget had a habit of rearing their head in the dark before bed. Until recently, she had survived by replaying her adventures with the princess over, but now…

Now, thinking of Arafrey made her feel just as glum as the memories she fought tirelessly to ignore.

Every stolen moment. Every glance. Every touch.

Did she regret their time together? *Never*. But she saw now how selfish she had been - and each memory only aided in adding to her guilt. Perhaps it had been fate that sent Reyla on a quest to save the planet, but it weighed her down with divine retribution. This was her penance and one chance at redemption. Nothing else should matter to her anymore, not even Arafrey.

Not even...

* * *

Reyla awoke in the scratchy bedsheets to see Tharin still sleeping soundly.

Already her shoulder was tight, as if tired from sleeping, a reminder of the distance she had to go before reaching the skills others had with the artes. She grimaced at the thought, rolling her shoulder awake before reaching for her gear.

Tharin crawled out of bed sometime later, rising to the sounds of Pudra shouting outside, his stomach contents sloshing with every movement. He kept his eyes low, speaking little as they collected their packs and left the inn. His pallor slowly faded as they hit fresh air and meandered their way through the village to the southern gate.

As they approached, the gates were wide open. Many Pudra gathered on the outside of the gate looking at the town walls, inspecting the damage left from the previous night.

Large scratch marks were gouged into the thick wooden planks. They were more concentrated at the bottom but expanded up, reaching just under a foot from the top. Sharp, wide claws had torn their way up the town boundaries where they met Pudran blades as suggested by the smearing of blood streaking back down the wall.

It was a grave sight, but served as enough of a distraction to allow them to pass by unnoticed.

* * *

CHAPTER SIX

Arafrey relaxed against the bathtub, closing her eyes as Ceal poured warm water over her hair. The water collected suds as it rained into a basin below.

"All clean now, My Lady," said Ceal, squeezing her mossy lengths. "You just relax. I'll get you some fresh towels."

Arafrey listened as footsteps crossed the bedroom, followed by the sound of the door clicking open and shut. She opened her emerald eyes to her now empty bedroom, her sight falling upon the cream robes laid out for her that evening.

She felt it strange to prepare for a party without Reyla - although it felt strange doing many things without her.

As Arafrey's aide, Reyla would have been the one fetching her towels and brushing her hair as she prepared. Back then Arafrey was too young to take a date so Reyla would accompany the princess. She was sure Reyla hated every moment, her duties similar to those of a babysitter's, but she never complained.

More recently, Reyla would have been on guard duty for such events. There was a running joke among the Palace Guard to give Reyla any menial and social tasks.

Reyla didn't seem to mind so much, but Arafrey was planning on returning the favour should she ever become queen.

It became such a tradition even Elsafrey caught on, insisting Reyla attend as Arafrey's aide in order to blend in more. However, Reyla owned very little in the way of formal attire and would be left borrowing from Arafrey's vast wardrobe of previously worn garments.

"I look ridiculous," Reyla would complain upon seeing herself in more feminine clothes, her hair tied back in hopes of taming her chestnut mane.

Arafrey always ensured Reyla received garbs with more subtle designs. She also made extra efforts to ensure the materials covered Reyla's shoulder so that she wasn't self-conscious of her scars.

She smiled, remembering the many ensembles.

"You're perfect," Arafrey would always tell her, often followed by a peck on the cheek providing they were alone. Although, she'd think so no matter the clothing.

Arafrey flicked her bath water, releasing a heavy sigh in hopes of suppressing the tears threatening to fall. She watched the ripples as bustling emotions bubbled under the surface, ready to burst forth at any moment.

One moment fury, the next unbearable sorrow, frustration building at the impossible situation she faced.

Her religion. Her parents. Her people. They were all to blame for the heartache she felt. She hated them for it. She hated them all. And she was angry with Reyla too, for running away from her emotions as usual. Although,

Arafrey had always known why…

They had come close to ending their relationship many times before. Reyla's unwavering loyalty and pathological need to do the right thing was severely incompatible with the intricacies of heart and religion. Even so, it pained her to think Reyla could end their relationship so easily over something the twins had said.

Arafrey was still hoping to catch Reyla on duty, but had yet to find her. She had even walked home past the barracks, but there was no sign of Reyla anywhere. All Elsafrey kept telling her was that Reyla had been reassigned - but not where to or why. When pressed Elsafrey remained evasive, and the princess knew better than to ask her father.

What was this assignment? Where was Reyla?

Arafrey didn't know enough to find a conclusion, but there was one thing she did know; Reyla was no longer in Ceynas. She couldn't be. The city wasn't big enough to avoid people indefinitely, of that Arafrey was certain; she had enough trouble avoiding people on purpose. Then again, that wouldn't explain her mother's behaviour.

Was it possible that Reyla had told Elsafrey of their relationship? Confessing her supposed sins in a misguided act of loyalty? Would they send Reyla away if she did?

Neither possibility brought Arafrey any comfort. Her eyes brimmed with tears as she poured over their last encounter in hopes of gaining insight into Reyla's intentions.

Arafrey jolted as the door opened and Ceal returned.

"Are you ready to come out, Princess?" asked Ceal, smiling softly over the towels.

"Almost... Just a little while longer..."

"Don't wait until the water's cold this time," Ceal fussed, leaning down to wrap Arafrey's hair in a towel. "Last thing we need is you getting sick before the festival. You'll never find a husband if you're all snotty."

"Wouldn't that be a tragedy," Arafrey replied sarcastically.

"Come now, they can't all be bad."

"No," Arafrey breathed, already defeated. "They're not all bad."

But they weren't Reyla...

* * *

It was evening by the time Arafrey was dressed and leaving the palace. Descending the stone steps and crossing the courtyard in sober silence, she ignored her new guard as he shadowed quietly behind.

She trudged towards the Pavilion, following the line of lanterns and streamers sprinkled through the canopy above. The many layers of her robes pulled her down even further as the trail dragged along the forest floor.

The Summer's Night Festival marked the last day of summer. The whole of Freya celebrated the changing of the seasons together. They prayed to the Life Tree as thanks for the prosperity the past year and made offerings to the forest for more in the year ahead.

A chorus of "Good evening, Princess" followed her path. Citizens bowed their heads, parroting greetings in their finest attire.

While the festival was in full swing, it seemed to Arafrey that the atmosphere wasn't quite what it used to be, the energy was muted somehow. Each Frey she passed made sure to smile her way, but it felt forced, as if they were struggling to keep up appearances.

Arafrey herself held tight to her facade. She would never let her people see the pain she felt, making sure to return the pleasantries as she wandered towards the Pavilion. After all, it was her role as princess to light the way as they prayed for their future. Even if she could feel her own slipping away.

The Cross Road Pavilion was grown from four white trees; the branches arte-formed to create a wild woven roof. Orange lanterns hung from the ceiling, giving the dance-floor an auburn glow. Yellow streamers wrapped around the trunks towards the pavilion-floor where Frey danced to the music.

Arafrey collected a glass of wine from a server as she dawdled around the outskirts of the dance-floor. She always found people were less likely to ask you to dance when you had a glass in your hand, so she was always sure to have one. However, as she was approaching her starting point, a friendly face emerged from the masses.

"You absolutely must save me, Princess." A Frey with flaxen hair in fine robes confiscated her glass, taking her by the hand. "My mother is on the warpath. She heard I arrived on my own again."

Arafrey near choked on her response as Bodair whisked her into the centre of the dance-floor.

Bodair was the first son of the Asrich family, known for creating the finest clocks in the whole of Alamantra. He was not so keen on clocks himself, instead choosing to pursue philosophy and become an author. Although, he had written few philosophical works recently and made quite the name for himself as a playwright.

"She just spotted me when I saw you!" he whispered, pulling the surprised princess into a dancer's embrace.

The two swayed in time with the music. Masses of well-dressed Frey surrounded them as they waltzed deeper into the crowd. Bodair glanced over Arafrey's shoulder to see whether his mother had followed him.

"Phew, I think we're safe." He grinned, coppery eyes scanning the crowds to be sure. "No Reyla tonight?"

"Not tonight," mumbled Arafrey, averting her gaze. "What about you? The rumour mill said you were bringing Tilda."

"Ha! I only said that so I wouldn't be pestered into inviting Tierin," Bodair scoffed. "Besides, if I come alone, I get to dance with you, and the twins might leave me alone for a week or two. Perhaps, we should get married and then maybe they'd leave us both be. Although, thinking about it, I don't quite like the idea of being king very much either."

The song finished, leaving Arafrey's laughter to fill in the silence.

It was not common knowledge, but she knew Bodair had a fondness for men and, like herself, was feeling the pressure from his parents to get married and procreate. She and Reyla had escaped from a party one night, some years ago, to find Bodair with one of the servers . Naturally they kept his secret, but were never honest about why they were there themselves to begin with.

The music returned, curious eyes on them as Bodair took her hand to continue dancing.

"Have you decided what you're going to do yet?" she asked, hoping his solution would bring her hope or inspiration. Like Arafrey, Bodair felt it better to suffer his parents' scorn than toy with the emotions of others.

"The time where I can remain an eligible bachelor is fast coming to an end, but as a scholar by trade, I figure I could just become an eccentric and throw myself into my work. I could always take on an assistant or find a servant boy in need of some guidance." He winked. "What about you? Have you decided who will be so blessed as to become your king?"

"Blessed," she mocked. "About as blessed as a hog in Pudron."

Bodair grinned, spinning Arafrey around and under his arm with the music. He pulled her back into a dancer's embrace before continuing on with the rest of the crowd.

The two bonded over their fuming parents, although Arafrey never told him how alike their struggles were. She knew he, more than most, would be accepting of her relationship with Reyla, but still she was hesitant.

"By the way. Did you see? No Marquel tonight," Bodair hushed his tone to disguise his contempt.

"What a blessing. I wonder why he isn't here."

"Didn't you hear? He's marrying Collette now. Announced it the other day," he snickered, his coppery eyes sparking with juicy gossip. "You know she was supposed to be marrying that noble guard of yours, the handsome one. What was his name?"

"You mean Tharin?" There had been several nobles on her guard over the years but only one ever caught Bodair's fancy. "He's been dating Dalliah for years now, Collette was the only one who believed that marriage was ever going to happen. Besides, those two are a perfect match."

"Isn't that the truth."

"May the gods be with their poor children," Arafrey prayed in jest.

"Children? Heck, I'd pray for their wedding planner!"

* * *

Arafrey became aware of her father watching them dancing under the orange lanterns of the pavilion.

He waited for them to leave the dance-floor before making his approach.

"How are you, dear?" he asked, placing his hand softly on her back, his face expressionless as always.

"Very well, Father, thank you." She smiled politely.

"I'm glad to see you, your mother wasn't sure you would be able to make it." He looked past Arafrey to Bodair, who hadn't managed to get far before his mother caught him. Galafrey's mahogany eyes slid back to Arafrey. "You know, you could do worse than Bodair…"

"He has about as much interest in the throne as you have in steak." Arafrey waved her hand. "I'm not sure he would make a good king anyway."

"You keep stalling, there won't be anyone left to become king. You know Councillor Irodent's son is getting married?"

Arafrey managed to swallow her disdain, but didn't respond. Her father took this as his cue to list all the many Frey he felt most suited to becoming king - not that he could mention any of them by name.

There was the son of the trader, the nephew of a prominent politician, and an expert marksman, each with their own impeccable lineage. Although not of noble birth, there was even a Frey who expanded his parents' simple shop into a vast trading empire. He was fast becoming the talk of the town. She would have to make her move quickly before he was snapped up, of course.

Galafrey then went on to tell her how much he was looking forward to retiring and watching her become queen. How he knew she would make them all proud and lead their people to even greater heights.

He had so many expectations.

For a man of very little facial expression and monotone voice, Galafrey was certainly skilled at letting her know how he was feeling without actually having to say it. All Arafrey could hear was his disappointment - and she really didn't need a reminder of the pressures she was under.

"You'll have to make your decision soon. You can't keep holding out for perfect, Ara," he warned as she turned to leave. "This is real life after all, not some fairy tale."

Arafrey pressed her tongue against her teeth and made a quick exit, her guard following behind. Quietly fuming to herself, she marched back to the palace.

How very dare he? Arafrey fumed. She never liked fairy tales. If her father paid any attention to anything other than his precious military, then perhaps he would know that.

Frey fairy tales often involved a helpless princess waiting to be saved by her knight in shining armour, which Arafrey took personally. Even as a child, Arafrey was adamant she would save herself should anyone ever lock her in a tower or dungeon. Although, Arafrey would be sure not to get caught in the first place.

The last fairy tale she ever read was *'The Tale of the Pigeon King'*. It was a Frey classic where a man makes a pact with a pigeon so that it may teach him to fly and scale a tall tower to save his princess.

She was fourteen, sitting on a bench in the palace gardens as the sun shone through the canopy. Birdsong chimed all around her and Reyla shadowed quietly behind in a navy dress and white apron.

"You know the issue with this story," Arafrey started, holding the book in one hand as she peered over the cover to Reyla. "This prince decided he's going to take it upon himself to save the princess, so she will become his wife, when no one has even seen the poor girl in years. He's just going on blind faith that she is beautiful and will be the perfect wife for him."

Arafrey was unable to explain why these fairy tales ruffled her feathers so, but they were just one more in a long string of growing annoyances. Her mother blamed her blossoming womanhood and her father seemed not to notice at all, leaving Arafrey battling against the tide of a whole plethora of emotions she was unable to explain.

"It's all hearsay too, no one has ever actually seen this princess. She could be dead for all they know!"

Reyla smirked in quiet agreement. After all, she was harbouring many of the same confused feelings as Arafrey.

"Not to mention, it's totally unrealistic for anyone to go to such lengths for someone they've never met."

"How is that any different to your suitors?" Reyla finally asked, distaste in her tone.

"I suppose it isn't. Perhaps it even strengthens my argument," admitted Arafrey, inexplicably hurt by the question. "My suitors don't know me. It's the crown they want, not me, and frankly that's what hurts the most."

"Anyone who knows you only grows to love you more each day," Reyla assured her. "Only fools would value the crown higher than your affection."

"Then by that logic, you must love me most of all."

Arafrey flicked her eyes to gauge Reyla's reaction, but as always, her face remained unchanged, her hazel eyes surveying their surroundings.

"Perhaps," admitted Reyla, emotionless. "You'll see. When the right man comes along, it will all just fall into place. You'll look back one day and wonder why you were ever so worried to begin with."

It likely pained Reyla to say the words as much as it pained Arafrey to hear them, each oblivious to the feelings of the other. Each trying their best to carry on as normal.

Deep down, Arafrey was confused. She had never had these feelings before and was unsure what they meant. In many ways, Arafrey had always considered Reyla part of her family, but the feelings she held were not the same as the love she felt for her parents. Although she knew of platonic love, Arafrey had few friends for comparison and found none as appealing as Reyla.

"What if I never find my king?" Arafrey whimpered. "What if no man ever makes my heart flutter or even meets my expectations. Am I to marry any old oaf? Or perhaps I'm to sit withering alone in my castle, waiting to be saved as all the tales go?"

"You won't be alone." Reyla flashed her trademark smile. "I'll always be here."

Arafrey smiled back, looking to the only friend she had ever really known - and wondering whether Reyla even liked her or if she only put up with her because she was the princess. She often wondered if anyone actually liked her or if they were just humouring her, yet somehow the idea Reyla was doing it hurt far more.

"Well then, I suppose I don't need this anymore, do I?" Arafrey declared, activating her artes as she marched over to the pond. The book still firmly in her glowing hand, she used her artes to loosen the bindings.

"Farewell, dear Pigeon King. I'm glad you got your happy ending," she called, tossing the book into the air, her hands spread wide, still glowing, as the scattered pages burst into thousands of tiny pieces of green confetti.

"You know, someone'll have to clear that up," quipped Reyla standing beside her. The pair watched as the confetti continued to fall, much of it settling on top of the pond, only to be eaten by fish.

Arafrey was reminded of that day once more as fireworks filled the skies around the Life Tree, the embers falling like yellow flecks of confetti. She held her head low as she entered the palace and stalked the halls to her bedroom. Ceal helped her undress before vanishing to join the festivities herself.

Alone once again, Arafrey collapsed on to her bed, burying her head in the pillows.

Perhaps it would be much easier for her to bow down to conventions and marry a man of her father's choosing, but that wasn't what she wanted. There was no man capable of making her heart flutter. No prince to sweep her off her feet. Of that she was certain.

Arafrey always knew the path she walked would be arduous, but it never felt like such a chore with Reyla around. A solitary candle burning through an otherwise bleak existence, Reyla had always been there. Arafrey felt so unbearably vulnerable without her, but she was unwilling to give in just yet. She refused to let go.

Even if Reyla was ready to give up, Arafrey would fight for both of them. She was determined.

Although, there was a small voice in the back of her mind that whispered:

'You know she's right.

You know she's right.'

* * *

CHAPTER SEVEN

From Everham, Reyla and Tharin continued south. The pull of their rings slowly grew stronger and more defined as they crossed into wyvern territory.

It wasn't an ever-present feeling, nor even anything physical, but whenever they were uncertain or even pondered which way to turn, they would suddenly become aware of this pull on their hand. Although it was faint at first, the more they continued south, the stronger this feeling became, and the more they felt it guiding them. Guiding them towards the volcanoes.

A warm breeze brushed past them, carrying with it more ash that clung to their clothes and green skin, leaving them filthy. Crows circled overhead, jet black against the clear skies, as they entered the remnant of a long-abandoned village along the volcano path.

It was a haunting shell of its former self. The crooked wooden buildings were greyed and splintering, their windows boarded up with misshapen planks. Fences were broken, shop fronts shattered and signs hung off their hinges, their inks long faded and impossible to read.

"We should spend the night," suggested Reyla, making note of fresh paw prints in the dust around them.

She had been worried about their safety since Everham. So far, they had little cause for concern, but it was growing increasingly risky to camp out in the open now they had passed into wyvern territory. Besides, she was still unsure what Toya had meant when he said the animals were more ferocious.

Did that mean they would be unresponsive to Frey artes? Or were they simply fighting back against the Pudra who hunted them for sport? Either way, Reyla didn't fancy her chances against a wyvern.

They sought shelter in one of the houses, barricading themselves in a small room to the back with only one window.

Despite the window being closed, the whole room was covered with a thick layer of dust and soot from the volcano, combining to make a thick grey powder. Even spiderwebs caught ash, their long tendrils reaching over the bare walls like fabric. Only a dresser and a bed-frame remained, but neither looked sturdy enough to use.

The two Frey unpacked their bedrolls to the sound of groaning floorboards. The sun settled as each reached into their packs for food.

"I hope someone let my family know we're on a mission. I'm sure they'll be worried by now. We should probably check in on them on our way back through Freya if we can," said Tharin, eating the grapes they had bought in Everham. "You wanna check in on anyone while we're there?"

"Not really..." she replied, averting her eyes to spy purple skies through their boarded window.

There was one person Reyla would like to visit, but she wouldn't – she wouldn't even entertain the notion.

"Come to think of it, I've never seen you with anyone, Reyla. Why is that?" mumbled Tharin, his mouth filled with grapes.

Reyla's heart skipped, surprised at the question. Her blood ran cold as she realised she didn't have an answer. She stuttered frantically but was saved when a howl sounded from somewhere north, answered by another due west, interrupting the conversation. They fell silent, their ears twitching at the movement outside, affording Reyla the chance to think.

Her first instincts were to lie or simply say she didn't know. Although, Tharin may take that as his cue to offer up a suggestion or worse, propose a solution. A lie would be easiest, but at that moment her mind was blank.

It occurred to her that she could always tell him the truth, that she had only ever had eyes for one person. If she were going to tell anyone her secret, it would be Tharin. But as she imagined saying the words, her heart stopped, knowing them to be false.

It was easy to convince herself the reason no one caught her eye was Arafrey, but it was just one in a long series of lies she convinced herself of.

Deep down, Reyla knew the real reason. She had always known.

A chill ran down her spine as her thoughts skipped over the waters of her memories agitating a truth long banished to their darkness. Unable to gaze directly into the void, her chest tightened as the demons within growled, clawing to enter her consciousness.

"See, I reckon most the guys in the Palace Guard are intimidated by you," Tharin continued. "You could kick the arse of any one of them *and* you have better credentials."

Reyla forced a chuckle, looking to the ground in shame as she acknowledged the beast haunting her. She was unwilling to share her darkness with one so pure, as if she were afraid that giving it a voice would make her weaker somehow.

"Shame though too, I bet you'd make a great wife." Tharin swallowed bread with a wide smile.

"You think so?" she asked, her thoughts lingering on the demons she tried hopelessly to ignore.

"Well, you were an aide, so you can cook and clean. Plus you're a soldier and could protect your kids whenever your husband was away." He shovelled some bread into his mouth before adding, "Kinda win-win if you think about it!"

Reyla studied her friend, clueless as he was.

In all the years she had known him, Tharin always had a smile on his face. Somehow, his caramel hair was always tidy, and his perennial-blue eyes shone with the kind of ignorant happiness Reyla could only dream of.

He was so innocent, a chick in a world full of vipers. Who was she to take that from him? Who was she to tell him of the real monsters of the world? *How could she?*

No. Her shadow was hers and hers alone to bear.

Again, there came a howl from outside, this time closer, followed by hurried paw pads and a deafening roar. The two Frey caught their breath, nervous eyes darting to the window.

The roar was different. Angry. Cruel. It rumbled like thunder, hanging tense in the air long after it was released.

"You think that's a wyvern?" whispered Tharin.

Reyla nodded, her eyes still fixed on the window, but neither dared move closer to check.

The roar came again, this time accompanied by the deep rhythmic beating of thick wings above their dwelling.

The house now felt much more like a shack and much less suitable to save them from the beasts outside. The walls flustered as the wings drew closer and closer.

From outside, there came a crash as the brute made contact with its prey. A high-pitched yelp hailed its success. Startled feet scampered by, dust kicking up to obscure the window as their owners escaped the village. The giant wings sprang back to life, the shack rattling with every movement.

Reyla ran to the window, peeking out just in time to catch the silhouette of a mighty wyvern against the moon.

"You don't think we'll have to face one, do you? In the trial?" whispered Tharin, his skin turning rather pale.

"I hope not," she replied, considering all she knew of the Pudra. "Although, I guess it'll probably have something to do with fire..."

"And we get a blessing too," added Tharin, their

previous tension forgotten as they changed the subject. "Fire artes would be cool."

Reyla smirked, secretly worried her skills in fire artes would be comparable to her skills in healing.

"I guess we'll find out when we get there…" she said.

'*If* we get there…' she thought.

* * *

The steep incline of the volcano made for a difficult trek as Reyla and Tharin hiked up the rocky terrain. It was hot, only growing hotter the further up they went. The dry grasslands soon became a barren, black-brown wasteland, as the rocks grew bigger and the air thinner.

In total, it took four arduous days for them to reach the top of the volcano - and what they found gave them little to celebrate.

Upon a large plateau stood a temple of stone with a wonky square face. A wide bridge crossed a slow-moving pool of lava allowing them to cross, however, the lava appeared to have risen in the Pudra's absence, leaving it to eat away at the plateau, causing the bridge and temple to crumble. The once magnificent building had collapsed where the platform had broken away, leaving behind a barely recognisable structure of three deteriorated walls and half a roof. Above them, the mystic blue arms of the Manastream wrapped around the clouds, converging above.

This was definitely the place.

It didn't occur to either Frey to pause, their mission far greater than the risk of burnt bootstraps, as they pressed forward. Their faces were beaded with sweat, the heat of the lava warping the soft metal of their shields as they crossed the degrading bridge to the temple plateau.

"How're we supposed to find the trial in all this?" asked Tharin, pushing on the temple door to little avail.

"I guess we look for that emblem. I reckon that's what the witch was looking for when we disturbed them," Reyla replied, walking along the temple in search of another entrance.

"Over there." Tharin cheered as they rounded the corner. "Looks like there's a side door."

The door was broken, but lay open enough to allow them to squeeze through one at a time, once they removed their packs. The tight space led to a narrow corridor opening out into what was left of the temple hall.

Reyla straightened, unease pressing her features. The broken shapes of stone arches ran the outskirts, creating a frame around a square clearing. It seemed like the rubble here had been pushed to the sides, making room for a glass vase. Lava gnawed at the floor where the building had fallen in, but the vase was far more concerning.

It was almost three feet in height, a foot wide at most, shining ominously as a dark mist bubbled and swirled inside. Unlike most other vases, this one's spout opened down to the floor where the mist poured endlessly into the ground.

Reyla moved in for a closer inspection, spotting a black diamond-shaped mana-crystal in the centre of the vase. She flicked the glass, a deep pang echoing through the broken temple as she watched the crystal exude tainted mana at an impossible speed. The mana rose to the base of the vase before swirling around and seeping into the floor.

"Do you think that's what's causing the sickness?" asked Tharin.

"Would make sense, although I've never seen a mana-crystal that colour before. We should probably break it, smash the crystal to be sure."

Tharin agreed, drawing his sword to shatter the vase.

The glass glittered in the lava light as the sword cut through. A cloud of dark mana held on to the shape for a second, before dissolving into the air. Among the shards remaining on the ground, the dark crystal still oozed, a stream of black-purple smoke rising like an ominous warning signal.

Tharin swung his sword once again, bringing it down on to the crystal. Upon impact, the sword sparked - but the crystal held firm, the force sending it to the other side of the clearing.

As Tharin went to retrieve the crystal, a rough voice piped up from behind them. "You're gonna need something a wee bit stronger than a puny sword to break a magical object like that."

The two Frey swung around to find Igniros, the spirit of the first Pudra floating behind them. Reyla jerked her head back, taking in the ghostly figure with her mouth falling open. Like his kin, Igniros had a weasel-like face and red fur, but his chin was wrapped in a thick black beard, making his head seem unusually round.

"But how?" gaped Tharin. "We haven't opened the shrine!"

"Nor will you. The entrance has long been lost to the world and my challenge destroyed by lava… It's sad really, once the wyverns moved in they scared the Pudra out, so no one took care of my temple and well, here we are." Igniros shrugged with a hint of melancholy. "I shall give you my blessing young Frey, so you may use the power to destroy the crystal you see before you."

"That's it?" asked Reyla, disbelief across her face at the prospect of things going so easily.

"Well, I'm so sorry to disappoint you, but seeing as my shrine is lava-filled and I need you to destroy the crystal, I'm afraid it will have to do," grumbled the spirit adjusting his large brimmed hat with both hands. Reyla had clearly hit a nerve as he mumbled to himself: "It was going to be so good too…"

"Now take my blessing," huffed Igniros holding his hands out to the Frey.

Reyla braced as a burst of energy pushed through her body, wrapping around her entire being. Static shuddered her fingers as her ring rolled, forming a second twist. She straightened, her body seemingly lighter.

"How does it work?" asked Reyla, her newfound power dancing around her extremities. She couldn't wait to try it out.

"The mana flowing through your body can now be converted into flames," explained Igniros, his sagely words sounding strange with his Pudran twang. "As the Pudra do, you will be able to harness this energy into a ball, a burst or even a stream. With practice, you can focus your energy and do all kinds of wondrous things."

Igniros waved his arms around to mimic the action as he spoke, unable to conjure the flames himself. Reyla supposed he was enjoying talking, although even she would too if she had been in solitude for thousands of years.

"Go on, try it," Igniros urged, pointing to the dark crystal. "Focus all your energy into your hand and activate your artes. Ignite the mana in your palm, go on, go on."

Reyla spread her fingers wide, tensing them as her palm glowed white. She felt ridiculous willing her hands to ignite, but then her palm warmed, the glow turning red as weak flames spluttered to the ground.

"You need to push," Igniros instructed. "Healing is soft and cool, but fire is hot, forceful."

His instructions unclear, Reyla tried again, activating her artes as she imagined fire appearing before her. She pushed on her artes but pushed too hard, fire erupting from her palm at Tharin.

"Watch it!" he cried, ducking out of the way.

Igniros chortled, rolling his ghostly form in the air.

"Almost," he encouraged once he was upright. "Try again. This time, try to contain the flame within your fingers. Hold its shape."

They tried again. Reyla concentrated harder, pushing a little at a time, until the spark ignited. She tensed her fingers as a small ball of fire appeared in her palm.

They celebrated their efforts as Reyla turned as Tharin held a fireball of his own.

"That's the stuff! Just take the flame and hurl it at your target," cheered the spirit.

Tharin went first, hurling his fireball towards the crystal. His attempt smashed into the stone floor, scattering debris through the air.

Reyla, taking the time to aim (*unlike Tharin*), pulled back and gave a soft overarm throw. Her fire glided effortlessly into the crystal, shattering it into thousands of tiny pieces, which shimmered as they fell to the floor.

"Now that's what I'm talking about." The Pudran slapped his translucent legs, and gave them a wide toothy grin. "Now away with you. Your next challenge awaits you in Sheya.

"I wish you luck young Frey.

"Trust me, you're gonna need it!"

* * *

CHAPTER EIGHT

Nymati pinched her ebony lips, exhaling as she directed smoke out of the open window into the clear midday sky. Her ruby eyes surveyed the many Sudra filling the sandy streets below. She glossed over row after row of flat roofs on square sandstone buildings, stretching west past the river Ballish and into the horizon.

The desert had been hard on her people, the blazing sun and dry sands leading them into drought and starvation with little hope of change. They wore poverty like a uniform, their clothes pieced together with scraps draped over their malnourished frames. Her people were comparable to charred skeletons from a distance, their dark silhouettes gaunt and dusty in the harsh sunlight.

Nymati had made many attempts to subsidise her kingdom over the years, but it was a hopeless task. Turning the lower palace gardens into vegetable plots and securing trade agreements with Pudron provided some encouragement. However, there was little she could do about the weather as wells dried, materials dwindled and her citizens suffered.

To the east, the Empire troops erected an impressive camp. Tents with red roofs filled the normally barren landscape. Banners embellished with a sun of gold hung proudly along the encampment's border, marking their territory.

In the weeks since the emperor's arrival, Nymati had done her best to remain useful in the takeover of her kingdom. The emperor had sought her council on a number of occasions, finding many of their customs rather alien, and she had served him well. Although, she already feared her usefulness was fast coming to an end. It was only a matter of time before she lost her power altogether, and the emperor discovered their secret.

Nymati returned to her cigarette, the flavour seemingly bitter now Drazah was not around to scold her, when there came a knock on the bedroom door.

"Enter."

A young Sudran woman with dusty-blonde hair held in a long ponytail opened the door. She wore cotton gloves and the thin off-white smock of her staff, the open back flashing the black ovals of her hidden wings as she turned to close the door behind her.

"Ah, Saffia." Nymati smiled. "You have news?"

Saffia was the latest girl to join Nymati's staff. While she showed great promise, her progress was slow compared to previous charges, which gave Nymati great cause for concern.

"Yes. The emperor left the palace for the barracks with Sabutok," replied Saffia with a low bow.

"Inform me of his return."

"Of course." She bowed again before making her exit.

Alone once more, Nymati returned her gaze to the city streets. Her sights flicked toward the army's training grounds and barracks.

With one last drag, she finished her cigarette. Looking to the skies, she exhaled, praying to Anneke-Sun her son was in an amicable mood that day.

Although, she knew rain was more likely…

* * *

With a firm boot to the chest, Amynus knocked his opponent to the ground. He whipped his wooden sword around to rest under the Sudran's chin. A warm breeze tussled through his umber hair as he waited for surrender.

"I yield," cried his opponent.

With a simper, Amynus removed his sword and stepped back, victorious. He allowed those around to cheer him on, while offering a hand to his opponent. Amynus had taken it easy on the poor fellow, but played into the charade to keep up morale.

Unease swept through Amynus' conscience as he lifted the tiny weight to his feet. He always considered himself slim, but in comparison he was an overfed primate.

"Good fight," Amynus assured him, trying to restrain himself as he patted the man on the shoulder. "Maybe next time you'll get me."

The man smiled weakly in response as he joined those

on the outskirts of the sparring pit.

Amynus threw up his wooden sword, grabbing it by the blade as he turned to the onlookers.

"Anyone else fancy a go?" he baited, his shining azure eyes daring challengers to step forth.

The sparring pits were his favourite place to hide from his mother. She never ventured into the training grounds, and he could stay there all day undisturbed, far away from her badgering.

He had only just turned eighteen when his father left to meet the emperor. Upon his return, Amynus planned to join the great Sudran army and prepare for leadership, but he couldn't bring himself to serve under the emperor. Now, Amynus just spent his days sparring, building his strength. And his nights… Well, he'd get to that later…

Another challenger came to face him, this one taller with massive muscles bulging from his tattered clothing. Amynus brushed his fringe from his face, rolling his sword arm as the large man readied his own.

"Enough, enough," called a voice over the crowd.

Everyone turned to find Sabutok leading a small group of Dura toward the sparring pit, most prominent of all, the emperor.

Amynus' blood boiled as he came to lay eyes upon the man who had killed his father. He was drawn to the behemoth's polished armour. Fury grumbled in his belly, his grasp tightening around the wooden blade.

Had his sword been steel, Amynus would have considered making a go of it. He imagined for a moment, transforming into full Sudran glory and ripping the emperor's body in twain. His blood lust surged as he dared to envisage a scenario where he would stand the victor.

"As you can see, our men spend much of their free time training. Many are merely hopefuls preparing to join the army, and we use the sparring pits to weed out any substandard performers," explained Sabutok, his bald head shining in the midday sun. "Ah, Amynus, putting my men through the paces again I see."

"Yes, Sir," he replied, straightening his back.

"So… You're Amynus," said the emperor, looking him up and down. "I hear you're planning to join the army."

"I was thinking about it."

"I hope you do," stated the emperor, surprising him. "It would be a shame to throw away a successful military career over a duel."

Amynus didn't answer, his blood suddenly scalding.

How dare the emperor speak to him so casually? And who would have told him such a thing? Had his mother been talking about him?

He tightened his grip around his sword, the wooden blade digging into his palm as he fought the urge to ram it into the emperor's smug face. Amynus swallowed, his knuckles dark as the pressure grew.

"Now, if you'll come this way, I'll show you the barracks," announced Sabutok, breaking the silence.

"Very good," replied the emperor, "As you were."

The men surrounding the sparring pit watched as the group of Dura followed Sabutok away, towards their menial barracks. Amynus remained fixed to the spot, his eyes glued to the emperor's back, as his hand coiled tighter around the wooden blade. Until:

SNAP

The blade splintered between his fingers, the hilt bouncing off the compacted sands of the pit below.

"You heard him," Amynus announced to his opponent, discarding the remains of his sword to ready his fists.

"As you were."

* * *

It was dark out when Callius left the records room that evening. He marched down the sandstone corridors of the Sudran palace, alone, towards the throne hall.

He had spent the afternoon going over the kingdom's financial history to see where they had gone wrong, although he soon realised the desert was more to blame than most. A detailed map and census showed that, despite its enormous size, the Sudra were a lot fewer in number than he expected, barely two million, and the capital city of Halda comprised much of that total.

Many of the citizens lived along the coast or within range of the Ballish in order to survive. However, there were many smaller settlements in the wilderness, and more along the borders where the sands met surrounding grasslands.

Such wasted space, he thought as he entered the throne hall. A plan was taking shape, the cogs still turning as he entered the quiet hall.

Torches lit the columned aisle, and the room lay dark as he crossed toward the stairs. He passed by the raised platform before the throne without a sound, and would have made his way right past and along the aisle, if not for an earthy smell which caught his attention.

He turned to the source where Nymati lay upon the golden throne. She pressed her feet against the armrest, her head nestled into the one opposite.

Callius stopped. Craning his neck over, he pushed on to his toes. Seeing her closed eyelids, it appeared Nymati was sleeping.

From his precarious perch, Callius could just make out the slight rise and fall of Nymati's chest. He admired the satin sheen of her raven hair as it draped over the golden throne, glowing in the torchlight. Her tail flicked intermittently by her waist, drawing his eyes down, sweeping over her slender form to where a half-finished cigarette cradled between her gloved fingers: the origin of that earthy smell.

"You'll have to forgive Lady Nymati," came a soft voice he recognised as Aeryn's. "She hasn't slept much since.... Well, it always brought her peace to sit there before..."

Callius didn't respond as he returned to his feet, and Aeryn stepped from the shadows beside him. Standing in silence, they watched Nymati sleeping peacefully like doting parents.

"Do you know why the Sudran throne seats two, Sire?" Aeryn asked, her voice devoid of loathing for possibly the first time since he had met her. "They say, the stronger the Sudra, the stronger the parabond. I don't know how much of that's true, but no widow has ever served alone long enough to warrant making a throne just for one. I believe the longest made it six months before she…"

Aeryn cleared her throat, swallowing slowly as if trying to bury the thought.

Although Callius had little love for Aeryn, he realised perhaps he had been too quick to judge her. Until that moment, she had never wavered when speaking to him, a firmness in her voice, her back straight, a stony stare always set to meet his. He almost admired her mettle. She was just like a dog, loyal to her master and quick to bark. Smart and ever on guard. She bared her teeth, but had yet to bite. He wondered if she would.

"Tell me. Which do you think your queen mourns more: the loss of her king or her kingdom?"

Having lost his own wife, Callius knew which he would prefer. He remained quiet, his face unchanged as Aeryn glanced to Nymati, then to him, and then at the floor.

"Our king died with honour and will receive his rewards in the afterlife, none will mourn his passing," the handmaid stated. Genuine fear and concern flashed through the grey stones of her eyes as she considered the implications of her answer. "I think perhaps, you mistake worry for grief, Sire..." She paused as Nymati shuffled on the throne, ever watchful of her master. "...and we already buried our king."

Callius released a breath. He found it rather depressing to imagine no one mourning his own death. However, in one sentence, Aeryn had reaffirmed many of the conclusions he had spent the last few hours making.

It would do him well to keep Nymati on his side. Her commitment to her people would prove invaluable moving forward. Their commitment to her more so: Aeryn was proof of that. Although, he was unsure an advisory role would be enough to satisfy a woman of Nymati's reputation.

"Wait until I've gone before waking her," he warned Aeryn, stealing one last glance at the sleeping Nymati as he turned to leave. "I can't imagine she'd appreciate anyone seeing her like this, best to keep it between us."

"Yes, Sire."

Aeryn gave him one final bow as he left the throne hall for the royal chambers. As he climbed the two flights of stairs, a sense of calm washed over him. It was as if he were returning home each night, the lofty height offering peace and protection as he slept above his Empire. He had disliked his room at first, but much like many things in Sudra, it just took some getting used to.

It was far too hot and there was never enough of a breeze to alleviate the stuffiness. There was netting wrapped around his bed, yet somehow there was always a single mosquito who managed to sneak through. Even then, he could hear the acute humming of its sadistic little wings. But, despite all his frustrations, it was the painted ceiling which often kept him awake at night.

At first it had made him uncomfortable to look at. With his head on the pillow, he would stare up through the netting to the dark purple and black pattern. The colours lay in stark contrast to the sandstone, making it visible even in the dark. All the while he lay below, awake, alone in his discomfort.

He stared at the painting so long the walls seemed to bend away from his vision. The symbols flashed across the back of his eyelids. Callius would have ordered it painted over if he were planning to stay, but he was glad he hadn't, since that too had grown on him. Like a scary story shared between friends, he found something familiar within the haggard shapes - and something else he could not quite place.

For all the mythos surrounding the Sudra, he found them charming. Although, he supposed even a lion would seem inviting, should it conceal its claws.

* * *

Amynus went fifteen rounds in the sparring pit before running out of opponents. By this point it was near supper and he retreated to the mess hall with the rest of the men to scavenge some dinner, where he remained until evening.

The mess hall held few embellishments, furnished militantly with long wooden tables, uneven benches and a serving counter where men lined up to collect the meagre offerings. The food was barely edible and the seats uncomfortable, but the barracks gave Amynus some comfort and much needed respite from political drama. Besides, it was far preferable to brooding around the palace as his mother fawned over the emperor.

With supper long since digested, the men retired, each slinking off to the barracks after a hard day of duties and training. They dipped their heads or flashed a smile as they passed by, hollow offerings to their former prince.

Despite their occupied status, it felt as if nothing had changed. The Empire troops remained in their encampment unless instructed otherwise, fearful they would fall prey to hungry women, and the Sudra settled into their new somewhat familiar regime. Comfortable, the men were quick to forget their grief, as rumours of aid and supplies replaced their reminiscing, fast becoming complacent as they basked in the foreign rays of hope.

But Amynus wouldn't forget.

He would never forget.

Having recovered from his earlier matches, Amynus rose from the wooden bench. Determination across his face, he marched toward the exit, ready for the next stage of his training.

Amynus left the training grounds, casting his sights towards the palace plateau before turning west. He stormed through the vacated streets, passing by the coliseum and along the closed shop fronts, to the bridge crossing the river Ballish.

The moon cast a watchful eye over Amynus as he stalked into Halda's western district, known commonly as The Narrows. Aside from the main roads running from up town and over the bridges, the streets here were barely wide enough for one man to pass through unhindered. The buildings were built on top of one another casting dark shadows in the moonlight, the ominous aura reflecting the neighbourhoods none too shiny reputation.

It was well known The Narrows played host to Sudra's oldest profession, which is the same as many other kingdoms only with a slight difference. These establishments were designed for the unfortunate souls who had yet to find their paramour and needed somewhere to feed. However, that wasn't what drew him to The Narrows each night. He came to tax his mana reserves and build his stamina with hopes of becoming stronger and attaining a more impressive transformation. Allowing women to feed on him regularly was the best way to do this, although, he couldn't deny the pleasure.

Leaving the stone bridge, Amynus turned right on to a side street. Here red lights guided him through the dark underbelly of their sun-burned city. Stepping over countless lost souls, he approached The Dusty Lock.

There was no sign announcing the bar's presence, just a single red door on a two-storey building of the same square sandstone as the rest of the city. The windows were similarly small, allowing only an orange glow to escape them, but it shone through the darkened alley like a beacon, calling to all virile men.

Amynus pushed on the red door with confidence. He strode through the dingy bar to occupy a booth in the quietest corner.

The air hung thick with incense and liquor. Men propped themselves against the bar, spines poking out through their thin shirts as they curled over their drinks. The walls were strewn with faded drapes and smoke-stained tapestries that consumed the candlelight, making it seem darker than it was. To the side of the bar, a set of stairs led to the cheap and readily available bedrooms which he was well acquainted with.

"Brandy," he huffed at the clerk as she arrived at his table.

Amynus lounged over the upholstered booth as he awaited her return, scanning the patrons to see what was on offer.

Several older Sudra gathered around one table, chatting among themselves, but none caught his eye. He supposed they were spinsters or widows, and that The Dusty Lock was their best hope of finding sustenance. A few younger women hovered by the bar - several possibilities - but they had already engaged other patrons. Then again, he wasn't above pulling rank should the mood take him.

Choosing the perfect woman would be difficult on an evening such as this - and he was not always successful - but still he returned each night, determined to become stronger.

There were only three criteria he looked for when choosing a partner. Strength, because he needed his partner to tax his mana reserves. Discretion, because he would rather keep his business private. And finally, attraction because... Well, he was a young man after all.

A young woman arrived with his drink, her hair a dusty shade of blonde, tied into a long ponytail. She placed the drink upon the table, smiling as she caught his eye. Her tail flicked playfully to her right, indicating her interest.

"May I join you?" she asked, pinching her bottom lip on a single fang.

Amynus made note of a patchwork leather bralette and skirt wrapped over a petite frame as he confirmed his first criteria.

"Sure," he said, flashing a smile. He gestured to the empty seat.

"Thank you, my Prince." She sat beside him.

"Please," he scoffed, pulling on his drink. "I know as much as you that I'm no prince anymore. Amynus is fine."

"I'll try." She nodded her head with respect, wisps of dusty hair slipping forward causing him to study her face.

She had soft features, but her nose was slightly crooked, perhaps once broken. Her eyes were like pebbles of malachite, shining against her dark complexion as she looked to him with admiration.

"I know you, don't I?" he asked, lifting his chin.

"Saffia," she replied, her eyes never leaving his. "I just started on the queen's staff."

"Ah... So you work for Mother." His chest deflated. "I guess she's riding you pretty hard," he offered coolly, imagining all the many labours the staff were subject to. "Don't worry, Mother's always had a taste for cute things. Don't take it too personally."

"It's not so bad," she assured.

"I'm sure," he replied sardonically, sipping his brandy as he took a moment to consider his position.

He knew his mother's staff were fiercely loyal, so discretion was assured, at least from the general populace. However, he could never be certain Saffia would not betray him as Taldi had.

It was also a safe assumption that Saffia was strong; Nymati's staff were the best, hand-picked from thousands to only six. Knowing she was a new recruit also meant she was unlikely to be too strong. Although, there was still the chance she lacked control which could prove fatal. But then again, therein lay the true excitement of his training.

"So, Amynus," Saffia purred, sliding along the seating. "What is it you have a taste for?"

Saffia moved in closer, a hand slipping over his thigh. Her palm glowed against his trouser leg, the warmth of her charm calling to him through the fabric.

"Strength," he told her. "Power-"

"Revenge?"

Normally he'd scold anyone who dared to cut him off, but this time a smile clawed its way across his face. It was as if she read his mind. His chest tightened as she pressed her body against his.

"How would you do it?" she breathed, pawing at his

chest.

"There would be only one way," he said, wrapping a lean arm around her shoulders.

"A duel?"

"A duel," he agreed.

His pulse thumped at the thought, the talk of revenge enough to get any Sudran's bloodlust surging.

Saffia felt it too. She ran her tongue over her incisors, her nails sharp as she stroked a finger over his collar. Each touch caused him to burn. Her breath brushed over his skin, fanning the flames as she pressed against him.

"I hear you're a formidable opponent," Saffia whispered into his pointed ear. "I heard Sabutok say you were undefeated in the sparring ring. That you once tore a man's arm clean off."

Amynus grinned, knowing it to be mostly untrue and that Sabutok was an excellent wingman. But seeing the way her eyes sparkled, he really wished it were true.

"Let's get out of here," he suggested, downing the last of his brandy and throwing two silver coins on the table. He offered Saffia a hand as she rose to meet him, her palm soft as it brushed against his.

With a triumphant grin, he led her to the bedrooms above.

* * *

CHAPTER NINE

The sun warmed the sky as King Galafrey and High Priestess Elsafrey sat eating a breakfast of strawberries and tea. They graced a table among the pansies and lilies in the palace gardens, the Life Tree glowing above them, as they did each morning before setting about their royal duties.

Galafrey was not a morning person. Seated with his back to the rising sun, he read left over notices from the previous day. Elsafrey, on the other hand, was an early riser and had never been able to stay in bed long once the sun came out.

"Nothing much from Sudra yet. Whisperings mostly, nothing concrete," said Galafrey flicking through an abnormally large pile of notices. "Thankfully, we had few relations with Sudra, so it affects us very little."

Elsafrey gave him a wry smile as she topped up her tea.

She had very much liked Drazah. Although they had only met a few times, she had found him to be a reasonable man, and she mourned his loss. She wondered how Nymati fared, but tried not to imagine how she was feeling.

"I've decided to postpone my trip to Pudron. With the

Empire taking Sudra it's best I stay close to home," Galafrey continued. "I expect Sudra will keep Gabris occupied for a while though. From what I gather, Sudra is in worse condition than we thought – if you can imagine."

"Perhaps Dominic would like to visit here instead," Elsafrey offered, choosing to ignore what followed. "His company would do much to lighten the mood around here."

"He's due up in a few months." Galafrey's voice deepened. "Besides, I can ill afford to waste my efforts with social visits at a time like this."

Already he was beginning to feel the threat of the Empire. As such, Elsafrey knew there was little consoling him and finished her breakfast without much more of a word before walking to the temple with her escort, Mika.

It was still early morning when High Priestess Elsafrey entered the temple.

She swept through the quiet corridors to the courtyard, scanning each of the sleeping patients as she crossed to the manapool. Elsafrey knelt before the glowing pool, her hands held together, silent in prayer.

Elsafrey gave thought to her people and prayed for their well-being. She thought of Queen Nymati and her people, hoping she would never have to face such sorrow. For her daughter, she prayed for happiness and wished she would find her way. Of Reyla and Tharin and the divine quest they accepted so readily, she prayed for their safety. Finally, she thanked the Gods for her people and how they had come together in this time of crisis.

Since the outbreak, the temple had been filled with medics, guards and volunteers from all over the city. The additional support was invaluable, and none had helped more than her daughter, Princess Arafrey.

The Frey queen could not help but beam with pride. Arafrey always tried to get out of her healing duties as much as possible, but now she was volunteering and working harder than Elsafrey had ever seen. She would even stay past the evening guard change, which was wholly unlike her. However, there was a deep sadness which had taken over Arafrey since the sickness appeared. At first Elsafrey assumed it was the stress of the sickness, but as the weeks dragged on, she suspected it was something more.

"Quick, in here!" boomed a voice from the temple entrance.

Elsafrey spun to the source as a crowd passed down the corridor and into the wards. She was quick to respond, her head calm as she followed the men inside.

"Let me through," Elsafrey called through the uniformed men, taking command of the situation.

The men parted in a wave of red and green cloaks, allowing her a view of the bed - and of Nasir of the Princess Guard. The poor Frey looked as if he had been struck by lightning. Writhing in agony, his green skin burned red, flashes of static running over his body.

"What happened?"

"He was praying in the barracks," explained Gurrien of the Queens' Guard, his face pale. "All of a sudden he was on the floor sparking all over the place."

Elsafrey returned to the bed. "Nasir, dear, were you connected to the Life Tree?"

Nasir managed a pained nod of affirmation, his body shaking uncontrollably.

"You silly Frey," she uttered. "Okay, Nasir. I want you to listen to me. Are you listening?" Elsafrey looked him in the eye to make sure he could comprehend her words. "You've been hit with a massive surge of mana. Your body is in shock. Now, we can soothe your burns, but right now your body holds too much mana. It needs releasing. Do you understand?"

Nasir returned a frantic nod, his eyes wide and tearful.

"I know it's hard, but you need to activate your artes," pleaded Elsafrey, taking him by the hand and activating her own as encouragement. She managed a smile, a poor attempt at hiding her concern as she tried to decide what caused the surge.

It wasn't uncommon for there to be slight fluctuations in the Manastream, but nothing so severe. She had read of a few cases in old records which described the symptoms like manaburn, but there had been no instances of such a reaction in a very long time. Certainly not in her time at least. A stray thought wondered if this had anything to do with the poison filling the Manastream, but Elsafrey quickly pushed it aside, fearing this was another bad omen of things to come.

A sudden gust burst through Elsafrey's fingers as

Nasir willed his artes into action. He threw back his head, releasing a garbled cry as his hands grew brighter and brighter. The mana rushed to leave his body, pushing everyone away with the force of a typhoon.

Nasir's back arched to the ceiling as mana continued to flow. The temperature dropped near freezing as it filled the room, whipping around guardsmen and aides as they braced against the raging forces.

The pressure reduced as Nasir fell quiet. The flow from his hands reduced, the glow ebbing away as he dropped to the bed, unconscious.

"Treat his wounds," instructed Elsafrey, stepping back to let Sister Ester take over, her thoughts already returning to the implications of his accident and debating her next course of action. She half watched as a nurse took Nasir's hand in theirs to begin healing.

"Wait!" cried Elsafrey urgently, taking Nasir by the arm to inspect it more closely.

Now Nasir had stopped shaking, she could see it clear as day. His scorch marks were outlined with the dark marks of the sickness, the black tendrils stretching across his green skin.

"Why didn't you tell me he had the sickness?" she snapped at Gurrien.

"I- I didn't know."

"He was fine this morning," Mika insisted, a waver in his deep baritone voice.

"Are you sure?"

"Positive. He's in my barracks."

Elsafrey fell quiet, her mind racing at the endless probabilities that threatened her people.

Mana surges this bad were rare, but anyone praying to the Life Tree was susceptible. They were also near impossible to predict and even harder to prevent. Her only hope was that they would not become more frequent, but she needed to do some research before her mind would be at ease.

"Clean and wrap his wounds," Elsafrey instructed, already deciding which book she would start with. "I'll be in my office…"

* * *

CHAPTER TEN

Disguised in shadows, forces moved as three cloaked sisters returned to their Mother.

"Are you sure it was the same Frey you saw?"

"Certain," she affirmed, fists clenched to her chest. "We followed them as far as we could but lost them in Halda."

"We checked the temple," added the second softly from beneath her hood.

"And the crystal?"

"Gone. Although we couldn't sense it on them."

"There's no evidence they found the shrine either," added the first.

"We should proceed with our plans regardless," Mother commanded. "Cali, accompany Venta to Freya and return to the catacombs."

The two bowed their heads in agreement, but the third turned to their leader with determination.

"What about the Empire?" she demanded, her sisters tensing around her.

"It's true I didn't foresee Gabris taking Sudra," their

Mother admitted, a sharpness to her voice that warned them not to push her further. "However, it's working to our advantage…

"Right now, all eyes are on Sudra and tensions rise within neighbouring kingdoms. They would have felt safe with Sudra between them and the Empire, but now they'll be running scared." Mother's voice ripened with satisfaction. "They'll be so busy mounting their defences, they won't see us coming until it's too late."

The three underlings joined their Mother, relishing in the moment as they imagined their plans coming to fruition.

"Now then. You have your assignments, I suggest you worry about them and leave the Empire to me," she ordered, lifting her chin with sublime authority. "Inform me when the deed is done."

Without warning, smoke engulfed the elegant figure, vanishing as quickly as it appeared, leaving the three underlings alone. Silence filled the shadows as the underlings watched the space their Mother once filled, unsure how to react.

"Hey, Ren," one started quietly, scratching her head under her hood. "Is… Is Mother okay?"

"Yeah. Don't worry about it. She's just angry is all," she replied. "You'd be mad too if two Frey stole the blessings out from under you."

Her sisters didn't seem convinced, but she needed to keep them in line. As Mother's right-hand woman, it was her job to ensure as much, although she had worries of her own.

"We must do all we can to protect Mother's plan and ensure our efforts are not wasted," she tried, half hoping she would convince herself in the process. "We've come too far to stop now.

"There is no cause greater than ours."

Her sisters grumbled in agreement, each raising their hands before calling out *"Perictara"* and vanishing in clouds of smoke.

In the darkness, with nothing but her thoughts for company, the distressed number two couldn't help but wonder if her faith had been misplaced.

It came as no surprise that her sisters were unsettled; she felt it too.

She was a loyal sister, but found herself disagreeing with Mother more often than not since putting their plan in motion. Mother's actions seemed less calculated than before. Her reasoning became more erratic with every meeting, making her harder to read.

Was it possible her beloved Mother had lost her way? To underestimate the Empire was one thing, but their position grew weaker by the moment, and it seemed Mother had no plans of defending them.

Her stomach rolled with anger and anguish. She couldn't allow anyone to derail their efforts, not even Mother. They had come too far to fail now, but a multitude of doubts clawed at her insides.

She released a cry of frustration, the sounds echoing around the darkness.

They had no choice but to continue forward. Yet Mother turned a blind eye to the hurdles piling upon their path. Perhaps it was time Mother named her successor and stepped down - but even that gave her doubts.

Who would lead them if not Mother?

Who among her sisters was strong enough to carry them to victory? Who had the knowledge, experience and talent to take their Mother's place?

The wind blew from behind. Her cloak carried forward on the breeze as if encouraging her forward. A shiver ran down her spine as she dared to imagine herself taking the mantle in Mother's stead.

Who indeed…

* * *

CHAPTER ELEVEN

Nymati had found herself with far too much free time of late, so was sure not to delay when the emperor requested her presence. She hurried down the palace corridor towards her old bedroom, but hesitated as she knocked upon the door. Her hand shook as she reached for the handle.

She had not been back since moving out.

"Come in."

Nymati half expected to find Drazah slumped over his desk as the doors swung open. Her heart sank to see that not even the chair was there anymore.

The emperor had moved the desk over to the balcony doors, where he now sat enjoying the breeze, nursing a drink. He gestured, "Please, sit."

Nymati closed the door behind her. She swept across the familiar floors with a deep breath, preparing herself for the worst. Her back straight and shoulders set, she sat across from the emperor.

"This is long overdue, but I want you to know this isn't how I wanted things to turn out," he offered, looking at his drink as he swilled it around, his voice smooth. "Once he challenged me, there was nothing I could do."

Nymati sighed, her shoulders dropping as she looked to the desk in shame.

She knew as much, but it was herself she blamed for Drazah's death. She may as well have told him to challenge the emperor herself - and the knowledge ate her up inside. And now she was going to lose her kingdom too. She felt like crying, but wasn't sure she had the strength to do so.

"In a way, I think it was the only way it could have been," Nymati whispered, shrinking into herself, weak. Her heart trembled as her resolve faltered. "We Sudra are a nation of honourable warriors. We do things differently, placing merit in strength and action. Perhaps in besting our king in battle, my people will be more likely to accept you as their own… Maybe he knew that."

'Maybe it was the only way we'd have any hope of keeping our secret' she thought, desperation clawing at her insides. She was so powerless.

"Who knows?" She sighed and shook her head. "This was not how I saw things turning out either…"

At their current altitude, the sounds from the city streets below became one, creating an ambient hum which filled the silence between them. Their awkward pauses had become less frequent of late, but then again, they spent very little time alone.

It was at this point Nymati realised that they were, in fact, alone. Completely alone for the first time since the emperor's arrival. There wasn't even a guard watching the door as she entered, which she found concerning.

"Do you remember the first time we met?" asked the emperor, breaking the tension as he returned to his drink.

"I'm afraid I don't," Nymati replied, feigning embarrassment.

"My father brought us over for your wedding. During the reception, you gave a toast and had everyone captivated before even opening your mouth," he said fondly. "It was amazing to witness. Even then you commanded your people with such ease and grace, it was extraordinary. You truly are a gifted leader."

Nymati quietly thanked him, although the compliment was somewhat backhanded since she was hardly a leader at all anymore. She wasn't sure what she was anymore.

"I've been giving thought to how best to utilise your skills going forward. I fear you are much too valuable an asset to just let go. Besides, what monster would just cast a mother and two children aside?"

His tone was pleasant enough, but Nymati couldn't stop her defences from raising. Although, it would be a lie to say she hadn't considered the possibility of eviction.

"You may find this surprising, but I've come to respect you very much over the last few weeks. And I think I finally found an arrangement we will both find agreeable."

Again, Nymati thanked him, equal parts shocked and concerned as she tried to determine his thoughts.

"Through watching you I've come to realise that *I* am failing my people," he stated, his voice genuine but rife with uncertainty. "The way you interact with your people, made me realise that I alone am not enough. My people need more. They need a queen, a queen they can admire and adore. And not just a queen. I need an empress. An advisor. A partner. An equal to lead by my side."

Callius paused, as if waiting for her to respond, likely hoping for at least some reaction, but Nymati's face remained frozen, emotionless. Stunned into silence, she realised what he was building to.

"It's clear to me that you're a big part of why your people managed to survive this long, but *still* they suffer," he told her, his voice gaining conviction. "Together *we* can fix that. By my side you could ensure your people get the supplies they need. Medicine, food, tools, resources. As Empress, you would have a hand in the future of not only your people but mine as well!

"Just think about it," he burst out, excitement raising him to his feet as he threw his arms wide. "I'm the strongest of my kind and even *my* people tell stories of your power! Together we can do great things, *amazing* things!" His mouth got away from him, caught up in the moment, as his speech turned into a cheer. "And our son, our son would be the combination of Duran and Sudran excellence. The perfect hybrid. An unstoppable force. A true heir to the Duran Empire!"

Callius stopped as if scolding himself for blurting out that last part. But it appeared his rousing speech had worked as Nymati sat still, seemingly caught up in the moment as she looked out the open balcony door to the sunny sky.

"I would still be queen?" she asked, toying with her lace gloves as the future of her people hung in the balance.

"You would – well empress, I guess."

"And I would have a say in their future?" Nymati finally turned to face him. *Was she really considering this?*

"Yes." The emperor clenched his fists.

"And if I refuse?"

"Well… Then… I suppose I'd have no use for you. But that isn't what I want," he pleaded, desperate in his delivery. "I can always find another queen, that much is true I promise you, but I don't want another queen. I want a great queen, I want the best queen.

"I want you."

Nymati hesitated. Staring into his violet eyes, she imagined her future. Everything she could ever dream of was being offered to her on a plate. After all her hard work, salvation was finally within reach. But at what cost?

Was this what the Gods had planned for her all along?

Amidst her heartbreak and sorrow, shone a blinding ray of hope. A chance to keep their secret and escape the hardships of the desert. A way to help her people as she could never have before.

Besides, it was almost romantic. How could she possibly refuse?

* * *

DESTINED FALL

12 MONTHS BMF

* * *

Confident the Quest would succeed,
I underestimated the Sisterhood's thirst for power.
Fat from hubris, I cast my sights over Reyla and Tharin as
they returned to the forests of Freya.

* * *

CHAPTER ONE

Reyla relaxed within the comforting embrace of the Freya forests, the dry air and citizens of Pudron having left her patience threadbare.

"Are we taking the Freya Road back to Ceynas?" asked Tharin. They had come down the east side of the volcanoes on the way back, allowing them to pass through Haston and enter Freya via the Balray Road.

"Yeah, but there's somewhere we need to go first," she replied, silently praying she remembered the way.

Five years earlier, Reyla had been a part of a convoy escorting Princess Arafrey to an event held by some nobleman hoping to win her affections. As was already tradition on away missions, Reyla was on nightshift and had perched herself on top of the royal carriage where she slept uncomfortably. When suddenly the front of their carriage gave way, jolting Reyla awake.

Arrows whizzed past as Reyla's training kicked in. Her eyes barely open, she jumped into action. Sword in hand, shield in - She had no idea where it was, but she was ready and fending off the oncoming enemies within a moment.

The men rallied as Reyla joined their forces to fend off

a wave of hooded attackers. She deflected a sword, plunging her own into the owner without thought. Their carriage damaged, Reyla made for the door, flinging it open to find the princess dishevelled but unharmed.

"Quick, with me now." She offered her hand.

Reyla pulled the princess from the carriage, swinging her sword at anyone who dared cross her as she cut their way towards the thicket. The men of the Princess' Guard fell in line behind them, forming a barricade to ensure their escape.

She led them deeper into the forest, her hand locked around the princess'. The sound of battle was long behind them, but still, Reyla held true, adrenaline driving her forward as her instincts took control. She had to save the princess, nothing else mattered.

Reyla glanced over her shoulder as Arafrey's hand pulled, her energy failing. She brought them to a stop. Her chest heaving, she drew Arafrey in close, surveying the forest around them.

"I need you to trust me," she whispered. "Hide in this tree and wait for my return. Stay quiet. Understand?"

Arafrey swallowed, nodding her head unblinking. Reyla linked her hands together, boosting Arafrey into a tree.

"Cover yourself with this," she instructed, passing her green cloak to the princess. "I'll be back, I promise."

Reyla flashed a reassuring smile.

And then she was gone.

Reyla circled back to their carriage. She expected some of their attackers would follow them, but the further she skulked through the forest the more she hoped her efforts were enough.

They weren't.

Reyla hissed through clenched teeth. There were two. No, four.

Did that mean her comrades were dead?

She shook her head clear. She didn't have time to mourn. They hadn't seen her.

With dusk chasing her rear, Reyla stalked the men through the forest. Her feet soared like an owl between the trees, slick and soundless, but her head remained calm and collected as she drew in close.

Without sound, Reyla pulled on her trusty knife, sneaking up on the first. Her hand slipped over his mouth as she streaked the silver blade across his throat with a single slice. Blood spraying over the undergrowth, she eased his body to the ground before moving on.

The second and third were closer together.

Reyla swept through the dark forest between them, securing her bloodied knife, before drawing her sword. She grasped the handle, her face expressionless as she swung the blade across their backs.

Devoid of mercy, she handled the blade with skill.

With no care for the lives she took, she pressed on, her only thought: *protecting the princess.*

With a dancer's grace, Reyla slipped between the men clawing at their backs, turning to face them in a bloody pirouette. Her sword followed her momentum to deliver two strong final blows. One, two, across the chest.

The men dropped to the ground, dead, but not before one released a cry, alerting the fourth. They rushed towards her.

He was fast, but Reyla was faster.

She ran to meet him. Tossing her sword to her left hand, she pulled to the right, just enough to miss the coming sword. Reyla braced against the hilt as the tip plunged into the belly of her opponent, bursting through his back in an explosion of blood and viscera. The two collided, knocking the Frey off his feet. His body gained air as the sword carried him backwards before dropping to the ground.

Panting, Reyla wiped her blade on her assailant's cloak, re-sheathing it silently before returning to the princess.

*

Reyla found Princess Arafrey still clutching her cloak in the tree. She climbed in beside the princess, her breathing heavy. Reyla wiped the sweat beading her forehead as she settled – *or at least that's what she hoped it was.*

"It's okay, we should be safe now, they didn't follow us," Reyla assured Arafrey with her trademark smile. She mopped her brow again, *just to be certain*.

The princess returned the smile. She shuffled along the tree, allowing Reyla to settle comfortably as they nestled within the natural perch.

Reyla leaned against the tree trunk. Her head tilted back but her eyes remained wide open, surveying their surroundings.

She was sure she killed their pursuers, but she wasn't willing to bet her princess' life on it. Without knowing exactly who attacked them, there could be any number of foul souls searching for them.

So she watched and waited, alert, her muscles primed, ready to protect the princess at all costs.

*

Reyla looked to the night sky, her body cold and tired.

It must have gone past midnight. The moon lay shrouded in dark clouds high above the two Frey as they huddled in their tree. A cool breeze rushed through the canopy and along Reyla's spine, causing her to shiver. Although Freya didn't ever get snow, it did get cold, especially at night.

"Here," breathed Arafrey, offering Reyla part of her cloak.

Reyla went to protest but knew better, reluctantly

taking the corner. She froze as the princess shuffled in closer, hooking her arm into Reyla's. Unaccustomed to the closeness, Reyla held still as Arafrey rested her head against Reyla's shoulder.

Her cheeks warmed. An unfamiliar energy spread through her body, each heart beat filling her with excitement, but also fear and loathing.

Bile ran through Reyla's stomach. She hated how she thought of the princess that way. They were friends, she was lucky to even consider them that. It felt deceitful to think of her like that, as if the feelings she harboured were betraying their friendship somehow. It certainly didn't help that everything she knew told her those feelings were wrong.

Not for the first time (*and certainly not the last*), Reyla swallowed her emotions and returned her eyes to the forests below, watching for danger so her princess may get some sleep.

*

Reyla woke the princess a little while after sunrise.

She wasn't sure where they were but was trained well enough for them to survive and find a village, where they could hopefully find help. All she knew for certain was they couldn't go back the way they came, instead she led them north-east in hopes of finding the Freya Road.

"This is beyond outrageous," Arafrey complained as they trudged through the undergrowth. "Who in their right mind would attack *my* convoy? Who even would have a grievance with the royal family?"

Reyla focused on the path ahead. She had many theories, but it was common practice for her to listen while Arafrey vocalised her thoughts.

"You know," started Arafrey, pausing to duck under a branch. "I wouldn't be surprised if it were just bandits who got lucky…"

'Not so lucky once I got hold of them,' Reyla thought with an internal smirk.

"…Or perhaps even–"

Arafrey stopped mid-sentence as the two Frey stumbled out into a small clearing with a large tree in the middle, her jaw suddenly loose.

Long grass surrounded the tree and a soft luminescence emanated from its bark, not unlike the Life Tree only much smaller. The Manastream converged in the clear skies above, crisping the air with its residual power. Unlike the Life Tree, however, it held a large door and windows, seemingly hollowed out into a building of some kind.

Neither Frey had seen any other tree that glowed like the Life Tree and marvelled at the sight. Reyla wondered if the Manastream flowed through this tree as it did the Life Tree or if it were magical somehow, but thoughts were not a luxury they could afford. Her hand reached instinctively for her sword as they stepped toward the strange building.

"Put that away," warned Arafrey, waving her off. "We don't want to scare them from helping us."

Reyla didn't agree with the logic but removed her hand nonetheless, leading the way to knock on the oak door firmly.

The door creaked open a crack. An elderly Frey peered out from behind thick circular glasses, her green skin greyed and deeply wrinkled. Her coffee-coloured eyes flicked over the two Frey, inspecting them, before opening the door wide.

The woman was no taller than four feet. Her grey hair was tied into a messy bun, which bunched up over her ears so only the pointed tips were showing. She smiled, wrinkling her nose.

"Come in, come in. Suppose you'll be wanting a cup of tea. Least I can do." She ushered them through the door, closing it tight behind them. "Take a seat. Take a seat."

Reyla could only gawk and do as she were told, as they entered a vast library. Bookshelves grew from the walls; they spiralled up within the tree and even down into the ground below. Rows upon rows of old wooden bookcases and dusty tomes filled every possible space except for a clearing containing a kitchenette, several tables, a few chairs and a large fireplace.

The old Frey collected teacups from a cupboard and placed a kettle on to the fire. She guided Reyla and Arafrey to seats and poured their drinks before sitting across from them.

"So go on then, which book is it?" The old woman peered at them expectantly over her glasses.

"Book?" repeated Arafrey, her brows knitted.

"You came all this way and found this place, you must be here for something," she said, her voice hoarse as if unaccustomed to being used.

Arafrey looked to Reyla for assurance, but she was equally as confused. Their eyes darted back to the old Frey in unison. She chuckled.

"Chloris, Keeper of Knowledge at your service and this-" She gestured to the tree surrounding them, her wrinkled hands held wide. "This is the Eternal Library. That is why you are here is it not?"

"Err... No... We were just trying to make our way home. We're a little lost. You see, our carriage was attacked and we ran into the forest and–"

"Don't worry about being followed, this place is protected by magic. Not just anyone can find it. And to find it by accident..." Chloris trailed off, slowly pulling at the loose skin around her neck. "Well... Not to worry. Perhaps this is exactly the place you're supposed to be..."

Chloris invited them to stay the night and eagerly cooked them dinner. Reyla supposed she didn't get much company as she seemed rather pleased at their intrusion.

As far as Reyla could tell, no one had followed them and the library was safe, so she spent the rest of the day exploring the many wonders of the library with the princess. They were allowed to go most everywhere in the library, all except for one door on the lower levels (*it was locked but otherwise uninteresting*) and Chloris' bedroom which was off the seating area. There were books on everything in every genre, from epic tales of fantasy to graphic journals from historical figures, the library had it all. However, it wasn't until evening when the princess retired that Reyla finally got a moment to herself and had time to reflect.

All in all, she was happy with the way things turned out. Granted her comrades were likely dead, but she traipsed into the forest with only her sword and the princess and they were still in one piece. In fact, they were safe and well-fed, which she considered a win.

They surely had a hard journey home ahead of them. Without knowing who attacked them it would do them well to stay off the main roads, perhaps even avoid the villages. Still, they were days away from Ceynas by foot and it would be hard finding transport without coin or revealing their identities.

Naturally, Reyla was up to the challenge before them. She was ready for anything the forests had to throw at her. Nervous energy danced around her extremities at the prospect. It would be untrue to say she was enjoying the circumstances, but she was suited to the position thrust upon her. She was so accustomed to her bad luck, the stress felt familiar, perhaps even comforting. Then again, she was also rather excited to be spending more time alone with Arafrey.

Reyla smiled, remembering holding her princess close in their tree the previous evening. The moon and stars above them, huddled together for warmth, and she, Reyla, the valiant hero who saved her princess from danger. It was all so romantic.

A lesser Frey may have taken advantage of the situation, but not Reyla. No, Reyla was happy just to serve and protect. Even if that one moment was all she would ever receive, she was happy with that.

"Ahhh, to be young and in love," Chloris piped up from behind her book.

"You don't know what you're talking about," Reyla hissed, turning away to glare at the fireplace.

"*I* am the Keeper of Knowledge, it is my job to know," Chloris returned, still reading. "Your heart flutters like a bird trapped in a cage, I hear it pounding in your chest. I wonder, why of all your instincts *that* is the one you choose to ignore…"

"It… It's not so easy…"

"You spend all this time worrying about the '*ifs*' and '*buts*'…" Reyla caught herself glance to the stairs leading to the princess. "When at the end of the day you have been disregarding the feelings of the one person who matters…"

Reyla pondered Chloris' words for a moment. Indeed, she never once considered Arafrey's feelings, but only because she doubted Arafrey harboured any.

"I have read every book, on every subject and I'll tell you this now; nothing good ever came from doing nothing," warned Chloris, snapping her book closed. "I'm surprised of all people, you would lack the courage to follow your heart."

Reyla scoffed. She would face a sword over dealing with her emotions any day.

"Mock me all you want, young Frey. Destiny has plans for you. It's time you start paying attention…"

Reyla remained seated by the fire a while longer as Chloris returned to her book. She pretended to mull over what Chloris had said long enough for it to be polite for her to leave, however, as she made her way up the wooden staircase, she started to wonder.

What was her destiny? What was it her heart wanted? Who was Chloris to question her courage?

So many questions occurred to Reyla as she made her way up a seemingly endless flight of stairs, but by the time she turned the handle and opened the door, she found few answers.

Reyla maintained her silence as she closed the door behind her. She crossed the small room to a sofa, averting her eyes as she passed the bed holding the sleeping princess.

The bedroom was similarly filled to the ceiling with book burdened shelves. Guided by the moon shining through a single window like a spotlight, Reyla crossed by the bed and undressed to her base layers. She was preparing herself for a night on the sofa when a small voice piped up from under the duvet.

"Umm… Reyla…" Arafrey whimpered, her hair crashing down over one side of her face as she propped against the pillows. "Thank you for… well… I'm just glad that it's you here, is all."

"Any time," Reyla replied, equipped with her signature reassuring smile, but this time it was ineffective. It struck her worse than any battle wound.

Reyla returned to tidy her belongings with a sigh,

unsure what to say or do. The princess was normally such a determined and charismatic Frey that a smile of reassurance was all she needed. It pained Reyla to see her struggling so. She had to do something.

Calling upon every scattered fragment of her social abilities, Reyla moved to sit on the bed, looking deep into Arafrey's emerald eyes before saying:

"You're safe with me, Princess, I promise." Reyla placed her hand around Arafrey's, squeezing just to be sure she knew she was serious. "I will *always* protect you."

Over time, Reyla said these words many times, but not once did she ever mean them anywhere near as much as she did at that moment. A sense of pride and affection, love and unwavering devotion flooded her being. Her heart swelled.

Arafrey felt it too. "You would, won't you?"

"With my life." Reyla smiled, and this time Arafrey smiled back.

Reyla gazed in awe at her perfect princess. Her pale complexion glowed in the moonlight with emerald eyes so clear and wide as to catch the stars. Reyla's heart grew heavy, her breathing shallow, unsteady. Her hand tingled, the softness of Arafrey's skin warm against her own.

If ever there were a perfect moment, right there, right then, *that* would be it. In her heart, Reyla knew this. The romantic in her cried out for salvation, but still, she hesitated.

She pictured for a moment how she would hold on tighter to Arafrey's hand. Then leaning her head forward gently before placing a kiss so loving, that by the time she pulled back, all her princess' worries would fade away. Reyla thought like this often, but she never found the courage to ever follow through.

Reyla could face a dragon, a demon, risk her life or near die, but when faced with her emotions she, Reyla, was hopeless.

Thankfully, her dear princess was not.

After waiting for so long, no words could ever come close to describing their rapture in the moment their lips first touched. Years of longing and wondering ignited, leaving freedom and lust in their place, drawing the two friends closer.

Reyla's body ran with excitement and chills, lost to the unfamiliar warmth and affection of another as they delved into the depths of their most secret desires.

What followed could have been considered dangerous, frightening and tough, but for them the journey home was anything but. Nights under the stars. Days walking through the forest. Foraging for food and disguising themselves through villages (*with only a small chance of being ambushed at any given moment*). It was all rather exciting, however as they drew in on the capital a sadness fell over them.

"Until it's time to grow up," Arafrey promised.

Reyla wished they had never left the library, but even then, they knew how it had to be. She nodded her head.

"Until it's time to grow up."

* * *

CHAPTER TWO

It was the library Reyla led them to now, heading north-east from the Balray road where Arafrey's convoy had been attacked and into the forest proper.

"How come we're going this way?" asked Tharin, as they pushed through the undergrowth.

"We're looking for someone."

"But what about Elsafrey? She said-"

"I know, but she won't mind," replied Reyla, painfully aware of the orders she planned to break. "You have to swear not to tell a soul of this place."

"Sure," said Tharin, following Reyla into a clearing. "What's so special about– Wow…"

The Library was just as Reyla remembered it, with long flowing grass circling the tall glowing tree. She smirked as Tharin fell quiet, imagining her own reaction was not much different. It was certainly similar to Arafrey's.

Reyla dismissed the memory with a firm knock on the door. Tharin wandered behind her, his head tilted upwards to gawk at the treetop. The door creaked, a flash of glasses peeking out, before flying open.

"Reyla!" burst out Chloris, her arms wide, her smile wider. "Not just anyone can find this place, but to find it twice. You are an unbelievable Frey indeed."

Chloris hurried them in as she had before. She had not aged at all in the years since Reyla had seen her last, although she was still seriously aged.

The library was similarly unchanged, however, there seemed to be more books than before. Reyla wondered where the books came from. She also wondered how someone so old kept the library so clean. There was more to Chloris than she knew, but her questions would have to wait for another time.

"I was hoping you could help us," started Reyla as the old Frey handed them tea.

Reyla then told Chloris of their encounter with the witch, finding the shrine of Auldafrey and their quest for the Hand of Miera. She explained how the sickness spread through the Manastream and how the Hand was their only hope of curing it. And finally, she told Chloris of the dark mana-crystal they had found in Igniros' temple.

"There's just some piece of the puzzle we're not seeing," Reyla stressed. "I was hoping you could help us figure out who we're up against. Or maybe what the trials are. Anything would be helpful at this point."

"That is indeed a tall order," Chloris agreed, sparks dancing in her coffee-coloured eyes. "Perhaps if we discover what your artefact does, it can lead us to a 'who'. Although if the spirits decided not to explain, I can't help but wonder why."

"You think they're being deliberately evasive?" asked Reyla.

"It's possible," Chloris mused. "After all, you've already witnessed Igniros leaving the confines of his shrine."

"Auldafrey said he'd been watching us too," Tharin offered. "He said he couldn't see beyond Freya."

"Hmph. Interesting… I'll collect some books," declared Chloris, jumping to her feet with the excitement of a toddler. "Help yourself to more tea."

Chloris ran off into her tomes, feverishly pulling books off the shelves with the occasional muffled *"maybe this one"* or *"no not that"*, heard as they patiently sipped their tea. She returned with books in her hands, stacked up and resting under her chin; this was not her first research project and she moved with ease. Chloris then placed the books on the table, skimming through each before separating them into two piles.

With her research materials sourced, the librarian was ready. She returned to them, her face wrought with confusion and consideration as she debated with herself.

"Now then," Chloris announced, pacing before the table. "Let's start at the beginning.

"I assume you both know the story of the first Frey, but I'll recap the important parts so you can follow my line of thinking," Chloris explained, collecting a copy of their religious text and placing it on the table before Reyla. "It is said when Auldafrey came to Freya he discovered the Life Tree. He found that, through prayer, he could communicate with the tree. Anything he would ask for; the tree would provide. However, over time he became lonely, so Auldafrey asked the tree for a wife and the tree provided.

"We Frey have always taken these texts as teachings and guidelines. Metaphors if you will," Chloris continued, her wrinkled hands waving as she spoke. "But what if it were all true? What if we are descendants of Auldafrey and a wife born of the Life Tree?"

"So it's all true. How does that help us?" huffed Reyla, already on uncertain grounds with her religion.

"It doesn't, but I had a look at the religious texts of other kingdoms. Pudron, Estra, Puwhar and Sheya," said Chloris, placing each book in turn in a line on the table. "Each has its own creation story, but there is one common element, a common theme: the first of their kind spoke with the Manastream and it gifted them a partner."

"If that's similar then it confirms they were likely buried within the path of the Manastream as Auldafrey and Igniros were," Reyla suggested skimming over the five books before her.

"Exactly," agreed Chloris with a satisfied smile. "But that's not what's interesting here."

"Oh?" Reyla's eyes narrowed.

"Think about it. What if the tree didn't just give Auldafrey a wife, but gave one to his children too?" asked Chloris. "What if our entire civilisation descends from a mix of these beings and Auldafrey?"

"So, we're all part Life Tree?" scowled Tharin.

"In a sense, but more specifically part Manastream," Chloris smirked, her silver brows popping over her glasses.

Reyla remained silent as she processed the information before her. She knew the scriptures well, having studied them alongside Arafrey on numerous occasions. It was said that Auldafrey was a God who came to Alamantra to make his home. Did that mean they were part God?

"But what about the other kingdoms?" she asked. "Are we to believe the Shey and Estra were born of the Manastream also?"

"Why not?" Chloris shrugged.

Reyla scoffed, but it went unnoticed as Chloris continued.

"Now, when you picture the wife of Auldafrey, what do you see?" asked Chloris, returning their attention to the first book. "Is she Frey?"

It was Tharin who scoffed this time.

"Of course she is." He picked up the text to try to find pages containing a description, but Reyla already knew there were none.

She and the princess had studied the texts for hours during her time as Arafrey's aide. They had once asked Elsafrey why there were no descriptions of their descendants, but she had explained it away. She said everyone had their own ideas as to what a God looked like, so teachings left that kind of thing to their imagination. Now Reyla knew why.

"Placing that thought aside for one moment, I believe this confirms the location of your trials and also explains why the witches are using the shrines to inject their poison," said Chloris. "Now as for your witches, I have a few ideas." Chloris reached for her next stack of books. "Assuming these things are true, it makes several other things seem more plausible which I would not have considered before."

Chloris then ran through a list of legends and theories from across Alamantra until finally picking a small, ragged journal. She held the tiny leather-bound pages close to her chest as she spoke.

"There are so many accounts of witches throughout history, it's impossible to decipher which coven could be at fault. However, there is this," she said, finally placing the journal on the table. "There's a single account of a band of witches once discovered deep within the Freya Forests.

"The author describes them as seriously deformed and unlike any race he had ever seen. He goes on to talk about their living habits and rituals, but then, there's this."

Chloris flicked the pages with speed and precision. She opened them on a page with faded ink and a barely visible image of a womanly figure holding a shining object in her hands.

"According to the journal, the tribe told him they were on a pilgrimage to their promised lands. That their people were sworn to protect a powerful artefact," Chloris said, her finger unstable as she pointed to the pages. "This could be your Hand."

"Does it say what it does? What the trials are?"

quizzed Tharin.

"I'm sorry, no. Things like this are made vague for a reason." Chloris sighed. "However, I do believe it gives us a who."

"A who?" Tharin repeated, although Reyla had already made the connection.

"You think this tribe could be our witches?" asked Reyla in disbelief as she connected all the information. She frowned. "You think they're Children born of the Manastream, don't you? But that makes no sense. Why would they wish to poison it?"

"I guess that's for you to find out now, isn't it?"

Reyla could only laugh.

"Yeah, I guess it is."

* * *

Tharin retired early, leaving Reyla to relive a distant memory as she sat by the fire with Chloris reading in her chair.

She flicked through the legends in hope of finding distraction, but had long given up. Reyla relaxed back into the chair, dropping the book she was reading on to her lap.

"You may have grown, but you haven't changed," said Chloris as she put her book down. "You're getting too caught up in the details. Just like you did last time you visited me."

Chloris was right, just as she had been before. Reyla

was a soldier; thinking was not her forte. Overthinking, on the other hand, she was incredibly well-versed in.

As much as she was enjoying going out into the world with Tharin, she did miss the comfort that came from routine and following orders. And that more than anything made her uneasy.

There was a mindless comfort that came from her military lifestyle. It was so easy being a soldier, she just did as she was told, but now the responsibilities rested upon her shoulders as never before. Every road they took, every enemy they faced, they would have to live with the consequences themselves. Moreover, should they fail, she would have failed not only herself, but all those plagued with the sickness who were counting on them to succeed. Failed her king, her kingdom, her queen, her princess…

"You need to let go. Step back and look at the bigger picture," said the librarian, before returning to her book.

Reyla didn't respond. The old witch was clearly trying to lead her to some kind of self-actualisation, but it was late, and she wasn't in the mood.

What was the bigger picture anyway?

* * *

CHAPTER THREE

Emperor Gabris was crossing the throne hall on his way to the dining room when the doors to the Sudran palace were thrown open. A Duran in fine armour strode into the sandstone hall, his blonde hair parted evenly past his ears and a crimson cape dragging on the floor behind him.

"Ah, Tidus. You finally made it," Callius called, his arms open as he went to greet him. "Just in time, I was just heading for dinner."

"That is most fortunate. I've had nought but travel rations for days now," replied Tidus as the two embraced. "Would've been here sooner but a sandstorm kept forcing us south, so we hunkered down in this piss hole of a village 'til it passed. Not all bad though, I suppose. Gave us chance to sample some of the local cuisine, if you know what I mean."

Tidus wiggled his brows suggestively. Callius sniggered, knowing exactly what he meant.

"Come, cousin, we have much to discuss." Callius clapped a wide palm against his cousin's shoulder. "And there's someone I'd like you to meet."

He led Tidus from the throne hall, exiting to the right-hand corridor to the dining room.

"Ah, Nymati," said Callius warmly as they entered.

Dinner was already laid out for them. A platter of roasted meats and vegetables were piled on to the polished plates. The sandstone hall should have seemed empty with only two tables, placed end to end, yet the smell of food and pleasant company filled it like a hearth.

"Nymati Tamun, this is my cousin, Tidus Gabris," he said motioning to his cousin, causing Tidus to bow. "He is the second son of my uncle, the great Fellias Gabris, and fourth in line for the Duran throne."

"Third," Tidus corrected, restraining his tone to remain polite. "Uncle Marven passed in your absence."

"Oh, well that is a shame," he replied with little remorse; his uncle was a vile old man. "Tidus this is Nymati Tamun."

"A pleasure to meet you," said Tidus nodding his head at Nymati. "Such a radiant beauty, the stories do you little justice."

"Thank you. The pleasure is all mine, I assure you," replied Nymati, her hand touching the ruby necklace on her breast. "Please, won't you join us for some dinner?"

Nymati collared one of the serving staff, and ordered an additional place setting be brought for their guest, as they took a seat at the table.

Callius reached for a wine bottle, pouring generous measures into each of their goblets.

"So, when are you planning on leaving?" asked Tidus,

helping himself to some chicken-like meat.

"Now you're here, we'll be ready by the end of the week," replied Callius, taking a portion of redder meat, although he had yet to place the taste. "After reading your letters, I'm eager to return home."

Tidus had kept him informed of current affairs within Dura since his departure. It seemed all manner of foul souls had decided to leave their holes and cause havoc in his absence.

"I'll be taking only two hundred Sudra with me and leaving you two thousand of our own to distribute as you see fit," said Callius, having called his cousin to Halda to rule in his stead. "We've already broken ground on new barracks. They're still some way off completion but you can always tell the men to pitch in if they want to speed things up."

"And what of you, Nymati?" asked Tidus, now piling his plate with potatoes. "Will you be returning to Dura?"

"Afraid I've never been to Dura before," she admitted. "However, I will be travelling to Dura to advise the emperor in Sudran matters."

Nymati turned to him with a knowing smile, the ruby of her eyes sparkling.

They had chosen to keep news of their engagement a secret for the time being. Nymati feared her people would see it as an act of betrayal so soon after Drazah's death, and Callius wouldn't blame anyone for being suspicious, given the woman he had proposed to. However, they each saw their union for what it was: a way to unite their people. If executed properly, their engagement would only strengthen the Empire.

"I'm very much looking forward to it," Nymati added. "Although my son is less than thrilled."

"How old is he now?" Tidus asked, his tone genuine as a family man himself.

"Just eighteen," she replied, looking to the table as she reached for her wine. "My youngest is eight."

"Eight, what a great age that is," Tidus said. "And two boys, you are blessed. I have two girls myself, seven and ten."

Callius smiled, quietly taking in the moment. Normally a conversation about children would give him cause to think of his own lost child, but this time he found himself looking to the future. A future he had long given up hopes of ever chasing again.

His proposal may have been politically charged but he couldn't deny the doors it opened, some for the first time in years. He knew Nymati could never take the place of Marella, but perhaps she could give him something far greater.

His stomach rolled, the excitement extinguishing his long-harboured sadness as he imagined having cause to join in the conversation.

'*One day,*' he promised himself.

'*One day soon…*'

* * *

Emperor Gabris gave orders for his men to disassemble the tents and prepare for travel. Four days after the arrival of Tidus, the newly appointed Regent of Sudra, he mounted a horse and led the troops away from Halda.

Callius reined in his horse, prideful as he beheld the magnificent sight of his polished troops marching in unison beneath the scorching sun. A glorious convoy of crimson and gold behind four horse-drawn carriages.

One of the carriages was for Callius, the others Nymati, her sons and staff, but he always made sure to lead the beginning and end of the army's journey. Besides, autumn in Sudra was hotter than summer in Dura, so he was happy to stay in the fresh air as long as possible as opposed to the stuffy carriages.

Nymati had offered him the use of an elephant to take back to Rhoda with them. Although he was tempted, Callius didn't think the palace stable staff would appreciate it and so declined. It did make him wonder why he hadn't seen any elephants whilst visiting the barracks, however, he was beginning to suspect he knew what the mystery meat he enjoyed was.

Commander Raltz pulled a horse up beside him, his Duran armour shining in the sun. A man a few years his senior, Raltz had long gone grey and bore deep wrinkles between his brows which extended up his forehead, making him seem permanently unimpressed.

"I wondered where you'd gotten to. What news have you?"

"All clear from the Fifth and Third division, Your Eminence," Raltz offered with a polite incline of his head. "First and Fourth are still struggling to get some carts over the sand, several Estra soldiers requested new shoes be fitted once we arrive back home, and the Second seem to be missing a few members."

"Do we know who or how many?"

Callius flicked his violet gaze over the marching army to the ranks at the back of the line. He had stationed most of the Sudran recruits to the Second under Commander Danrock Hurlts, a Duran soldier with an impressive battle record. He had hoped they would respect him more than the other Division leaders, but news of deserters did not surprise him.

"Hurlts suggested at least twenty, although not all of them were Sudra," Raltz replied, to his surprise. "Would you like us to do anything about them?"

"No, let them be. Twenty is hardly a number to cry about and if our men feel they would better serve the Empire here then they are welcome to," he replied.

"Besides," he added with a baleful smile. "We'll be back here soon enough…"

* * *

CHAPTER FOUR

Autumn offered High Priestess Elsafrey little to celebrate. Nearly eight weeks after Reyla and Tharin left for Pudron, the number of Frey burdened with the sickness only continued to increase. Her attempts to contain the sickness were proving futile. In the end, she sent all the patients she could home, clearing the temple courtyard and wards.

For the most part, those infected grew accustomed to the scourge. Many likened the pain to old breaks or headaches. Others struggled with avoiding using their artes more than they struggled with the sickness, there was little she could do to deter them, but everyone was feeling the strain.

There were some unfortunate souls left bed ridden. The more severe cases, like Nasir, left Frey with their bodies streaked with the black rash and squirming with pain. Fortunately, no one had died, but the Frey queen knew it was only a matter of time.

Despite the sickness, things were beginning to calm down for Elsafrey as she returned to her routine. Having explored all avenues for treating the sickness, there was little more she could do now other than wait for Reyla and Tharin to return home.

"I've set some time aside for your studies after the sermon tomorrow," she told Arafrey at dinner that evening.

Although they spent much of their time in the temple together, they hardly had time to interact and missed many of their usual dinners. While her daughter was hardly social at the best of times, Arafrey's mood continued to worsen with each passing day. A dark cloud hung over her, warning Elsafrey away from asking about her social life, forcing her to keep their discussions light.

"How's your new guard working out for you?" Elsafrey inquired, placing her utensils on to an empty plate.

"He's fine," Arafrey mumbled. "Reyla was better…"

"Well, she did leave large shoes to fill." She knew Arafrey would have objections to transferring Reyla to the Queen's Guard, but never expected her to be so sore.

"Where is Reyla anyway?" asked Arafrey, toying with her food like a child.

"I told you, she's on special assignment." Elsafrey wiped her mouth with a napkin. "She should be back any day now."

Elsafrey had decided not to tell Arafrey the true cause of Reyla's absence. She and Galafrey agreed it best to keep the full extent of their troubles to themselves, putting their faith in Reyla and Tharin. There would be outright panic if word got out.

Elsafrey's thoughts returned to the night she had learned of the Hand of Miera. The image of her brave soldiers as they offered her a chance at salvation was burned into her memory. They had grown into such fine soldiers that even the Gods themselves thought them worthy. Her heart warmed, flushing with maternal pride.

Like a mother hen, Elsafrey had taken Reyla under her wing after her mother passed. Elsafrey had nurtured Reyla alongside her own daughter, teaching her all she needed to succeed in high society.

Elsafrey had always regretted her meddling, having resented her parents for theirs, but her gentle nudging had cultivated a woman primed to stand beside Arafrey as she faced the hardships of ruling. She dreaded to wonder how things would have turned out had she not called Reyla into her office that day…

"Have you thought about marriage at all, Reyla?" Elsafrey asked the eighteen-year-old aide.

She had not, although that was no surprise to anybody.

"The princess will need allies as she becomes queen," she told Reyla. "The king has his knights, but we women have a much more important role. If you were to choose the right husband, you could become a vital member of Ara's inner circle. Just think about it."

But Reyla didn't hesitate. "I'd like to join the military."

"A soldier?"

"A member of the Palace Guard. Perhaps even a knight."

"A knight? That's quite the ambition."

"All I wish is to serve and protect," vowed Reyla, her back straight and eyes determined. "Give me a sword and a shield and I swear to you, as long as I live and breathe, no harm shall befall our princess."

At the time, Elsafrey hadn't thought much of it, but looking back she wondered why Reyla chose to become a soldier. Why pass up on the chance of nobility only to spend your life in servitude? Risking your life for others?

Elsafrey returned her gaze to her still sulking daughter. Was it possible Reyla wasn't risking her life for others, but perhaps just *one* other?

Her stomach dropped to the floor as suddenly it all made sense. Everything from Arafrey's stubbornness regarding marriage, to her skulking around the temple to see the guard change.

A juniper smile crept over the Frey queen's face as she pieced it all together. It seemed so obvious to Elsafrey now. Her heart swelled, overjoyed to think her daughter had already found the love and support she was so desperate for her to find.

Elsafrey was happy with herself for figuring it out, but her heart broke in the same breath. A heaviness hit her chest to think her daughter would feel the need to keep anything from her.

Elsafrey had always considered them close, but it seemed she hardly knew her daughter at all. Her stomach lurched. How much pressure had they been putting on Arafrey that she would feel such a way?

Elsafrey cursed herself for being so oblivious. So

neglectful and cruel. She failed her child, her greatest love and creation.

Elsafrey was racking her brain in hopes of finding a way to show her support, when there came a knock at the door. A messenger made a hasty appearance, handing her a paper note and giving a sharp bow before leaving without comment.

"I need you to run an errand for me," said Elsafrey regarding the notice, her smile returning. "I have something I must attend to."

"What? Now?"

"Yes, now. Come on, collect yourself."

With a groan Arafrey rose from her chair, collecting her shawl before following Elsafrey down the corridor.

* * *

OMISSION

* * *

Telling it now, I wonder if the events that were to follow could have been avoided.
I ask myself:
What if that messenger came but one day sooner?
What if dear Elsafrey decided not to involve her daughter?
Perhaps if she did, things would have turned out differently.
But deep down, I know this was the only way it could ever have been.

* * *

CHAPTER ONE

It was earlier that afternoon when Reyla and Tharin passed the stone bears of the Ceynas Cemetery.

Everything was going remarkably well. They left the Library and traversed the forests with little incident, heading north until finding the Freya Road, where passing merchants offered them aid between villages. Perhaps that was why Reyla was so anxious as they passed the city boundaries and into the light of the Life Tree.

Ceynas was still busy as they entered the city proper. Throngs of Frey filled the worn forest paths and crowed around the market. Reyla pulled up her hood, trudging through the trees to a secluded inn in Low Town.

"You check in," said Tharin, grinning as he passed Reyla his pack. He brushed a hand through his caramel hair. "I'm gonna run home and let everyone know I'm alright. You sure you don't mind?"

Reyla gave him a nod of affirmation, shouldering his gear as he vanished into the forests. It wasn't as if she had anyone to visit, her parents were long gone and those who remained tested her patience more than most.

Although she doubted there were spies in the palace, it

was best to proceed with caution, so Reyla arranged a messenger to inform Elsafrey of their return while booking a room. She then hauled their gear up to the scruffy twin room, where she awaited further instruction.

By Frey standards the accommodation was poor. There were no dangerous parts of Ceynas, but there were poorer ones, forgotten ones. Places where no one would ever think to look for them - which was exactly what they wanted given the circumstances.

It wasn't unclean but it wasn't tidy either, everything seemingly old and scruffy-looking. Moth-eaten curtains draped over an open window, swaying in the slight breeze, yet the air lay musty and stale. The beds and dresser looked older than Reyla and she suspected the mattresses had seen better days. Even her bunk in the barracks seemed more appealing, but she had long given up caring where she rested her head.

With a deep sigh, Reyla dropped their gear and removed her armour, placing it neatly on the wobbly dresser. She ran her hand over her shoulder, the pale glow of her artes shining on her olivine skin with the kind of proficiency she had always dreamed of. Their weeks of travel seemed to catch up with her then, and Reyla shuffled to one of the beds, her limbs rejoicing as she threw herself on to the solid mattress. Resting her head upon the pillow, she stared at the cracked ceiling.

So much had happened it was no surprise she was exhausted. Her joints throbbed and burned. Before arriving at the inn, she could sleep for a year, but now she had stopped static filled her body – as if she were desperate to get moving again. It didn't feel right just lying there while there was so much to consider and so many problems to overcome. Although, experience dictated she should probably take any rest she could get.

Reyla tried to clear her thoughts, listening to the sounds of Frey chatting in the streets below through the open window. She smiled at the familiar chirps of cheddicks and bluecrests flitting through the trees above, glad to be free from the crows of Pudron. Breathing in the Freya air, she welcomed a bouquet of fragrances she found she had missed on their travels.

Her eyes closed as she soaked up the ambience. Fresh soil, lavender, pine and oak. It was comforting. Soothing. The aroma of home.

Reyla only closed her eyes for a second - but was rudely woken hours later when someone rapped on the door.

"Come in," she called, jumping to attention as she scrambled to arrange her base layers. "Sorry, I must've-"

She expected to greet Tharin, or perhaps Queen Elsafrey, but Reyla's heart stopped when she saw Princess Arafrey in the doorway.

Reyla's spirit left her body and she momentarily forgot how to function, so she just hung clumsily like a neglected scarecrow. Arafrey said nothing as she closed the door, leaving Reyla to catch flies in her hanging mouth. *What was she doing there?*

Arafrey peeled back around to meet her, a glowering pout upon her juniper lips as her eyes locked upon Reyla's. Their shining emerald beauty now sparked with hurt and betrayal. Reyla opened her mouth to say something, but nothing came out. Instead, she remained awkward and still, the distance between them growing with every passing second. Their hearts drowning in uncertainty and sorrow, each wavered, unable to tell the other how they truly felt.

"Mother said you were on assignment," Arafrey finally managed, breaking the tension with a soft smile. She tucked hair behind her pointed ears, holding the mossy lengths as her eyes dropped to the floor. "I'm glad you're okay, I mi–"

"I'm here to make my report for the queen," Reyla burst out, militant in her delivery, but her heart jutted forward, unearthing feelings she buried so callously. A rumbling of abandoned hopes rushed to the surface, trembling on the edge of her lips as she fought the urge to take back all she had said.

Reyla hesitated, ice cracking across her chest. She wished desperately to tell the princess what a fool she was. How it was all she could do not to think about her, every moment of every day. That even their almighty quest wasn't enough to distract her from the emptiness she felt.

But all she said was:

"I've much to report…"

* * *

Reyla did indeed have a lot to report, but while she debriefed, an unsavoury figure entered Ceynas.

Slipping through woodland paths unnoticed, they

entered the palace grounds. The sun grew tired as the figure snaked their way through lilies. Hiding in shadows, they approached the timber palace, clawing up the oaken wall to the balcony.

With a single swift motion, they propelled up and over the railing, finding an open door.

Thin curtains tussled in the gentle breeze as they crept past. They turned to the bed, the glow of the Life Tree casting a tall shadow across the floor as they stalked closer. They slowed their approach, watching as two Frey slept soundly in a grand bed of polished wood. Their crowns sat proudly on ornate bedsides as they nestled in towards each other. Unaware.

Bony fingers reached into a cloak, curling around a blade handle. The figure clutched the blade in both hands, raising it high above their head. They loomed over the sleeping couple.

It was at that moment, fate intervened.

The wind blew unusually cold, sweeping through the drapes and past the figure. The breeze brushed over the sleeping Frey, causing the queen to shiver. Her eyes opened as she stirred, just enough to catch the cold steel rising above her.

It all happened so fast. No thoughts flashed through Elsafrey's mind as the knife plummeted. Her eyes heavy, Elsafrey rose to meet the intruder. She waved her arms at the murderous shadow, pushing them away from the bed.

A flash of steel cut through the night like cat eyes. Elsafrey snatched at the blade as it swung, catching the figure by the wrist. She held it tight. Her teeth clenched as the figure whipped around in the darkness attempting to shake her loose.

Elsafrey recoiled as they hit her across the face.

Her nose bloodied, Elsafrey launched at the figure once more. Scratching and wailing, she forced them away from her beloved. Back towards the balcony. Planning to push them over, until–

Squelch.

Elsafrey stopped. An acute whine filled her ears as the world appeared to echo and move in slow motion.

She turned, a strange weight to her body. Galafrey was already awake, alerting the guards. He sped past, chasing the shadow as they escaped over the balcony.

Elsafrey looked down, her trembling fingers pawing at the burning sensation spreading across her stomach. It was wet and warm. Mind numb, she returned to Galafrey, the expression upon his face more telling than he knew.

Dread washed over Elsafrey as her knees gave way. Galafrey ran to catch her. Wrapped within his arms, they crashed to the floor together.

"Quick, call a medic," Galafrey barked at the guards, tears filling his mahogany eyes. "Sound the alarms!"

Galafrey pulled Elsafrey in close. Her eyes glazed over, giving everything a halo as blood spilled through glowing fingers. His eyes flashed, desperate as he failed to stop the flow.

"Please, Elsa," Galafrey begged, alarm bells sounding in the distance. "Please. Tell me what to do. It won't stop."

She hadn't the strength to help. His hand pressed firm against the gaping wound. The glow of his artes filled the room to little effect.

Blood pooled around them as Elsafrey placed her hand over his. Her eyes tear-filled, she looked up at her husband.

"It's okay," she whispered, her vision growing dark.

"Elsa."

A calm serenity washed over Elsafrey. The last time he had cried was the day their daughter was born. She flushed with pride, her heart full as her body grew cold.

"Elsa. No, Elsa, please."

But the Frey Queen didn't respond. She closed her eyes, her hands falling to the side as she smiled one last time.

* * *

CHAPTER TWO

Elsafrey wasn't the only one in danger that night.

The constant movement within the Empire's army allowed for a great many things to go unnoticed. Many men among the Duran ranks were forced to learn on the job and had little idea of the proper ways to do things. As such, things went missing, weapons were misplaced and people who had nothing but dreadful intentions slipped by unhindered.

One such person strode to the emperor's tent, a wine bottle clutched tightly in her gloved fingers as she approached. She quashed her nerves, her head high as she passed by the Duran soldiers on guard, knowing the smock and gloves she wore would deter them from making eye contact.

She found it humorous how uncomfortable the Dura were around women, but it worked to her advantage as she slipped by without acknowledgement or recognition.

Niggling doubts drew extra beats from her heart as she crossed the tent to the makeshift lounge. Here the two leaders intensely talked shop, ignoring her entry.

Rulers like Nymati and the emperor never really paid

any attention to who served them. So long as somebody was there, they wouldn't care - only if there wasn't anyone around would they ever really notice. Their ignorance made it easy for her to walk over to their table, where the decanter sat empty.

With shivers along her spine, she pulled the cork from the bottle and decanted the wine. Her hand steady, she emptied the few last drops in full sight of the two clueless leaders.

A smirk trembled on her lips as she returned the decanter and stepped away unnoticed. Nymati Tamun and Callius Gabris would have no idea what they were about to ingest until it was too late.

Essence of Noctinka, a potion that caused the consumer to lose their inhibitions and fall victim to carnal urges. Knowing Nymati harboured a lot of unresolved anger towards the Duran Emperor, it wouldn't be long before the sparks would fly.

She commended herself on thinking of it. They would tear each other apart by morning and there was no way to stop it once ingested.

It was almost too perfect.

They saw nothing. They noticed nothing.

Now to wait…

* * *

Nymati waved off the girl serving them, her eyes on the map spread over the table made of wooden crates between her and the emperor.

"There's little fertile soil that far west," she said, the emperor's plans for Sudra's redevelopment growing more ambitious by the day. "We considered diverting new rivers from the Ballish but there's no rainfall to replenish them and the Ballish will likely suffer."

"Perhaps if we connected the Leste over this way." The emperor crossed the map with his finger pointed. Even without his armour, the emperor was impressive; a lean slab of muscles in a grey tunic, which strained across his biceps whenever he flexed. He sat back, rubbing a hand through his stubble, his attention on her. "What about other income?"

"Sand's our biggest export. It's collected by the Vagre Outposts to the east of the Ballish, here, and Karanist the west, over here," she explained, running her long nail over the map.

Nymati stretched back and slumped into the cushion and crate furniture, glad to be free of their stuffy carriages. She was stiff from travelling, but still made the effort to dine with the emperor each evening. It was often tiresome but more entertaining than staring at the walls of her tent at the very least.

"We had an agreement with Galafrey to allow us free passage to Pudron, however, I would suspect that is no longer an option, given present circumstances."

"Why'd the Pudra want sand?"

"It's not just sand. The sand found in these areas is

lousy with minerals," Nymati replied, her tail flicking with pride. "It makes for much better glass than sand from the coast but is too fine to refine."

"And what about mineral deposits?"

"We have the mines in Tagrin, but they've long since started to dry up and the citizens up there are as poor as any. There was another mineral reserve, here and here." Nymati pointed to the map before refilling her wine from the decanter. "They were once home to great lakes which ran dry. We still find things, but very rarely."

"So, you're reliant on tax for income?"

Nymati snorted into her glass as she lifted it to her lips. "Who would we tax? The men struggling to buy food and clothes? No, many of the buildings in Sudra belong to the crown, they are rented out to the public as homes or for events and business. Each town and village contributes what they can, but the colosseum accounts for much of Halda's income."

"So, it's like an entertainment tax?"

She laughed. "I've never thought about it like that before."

Nymati caught herself smiling but pressed it away to sip her wine. She made note of the unfamiliar but sweet vintage and wondered if they were drinking Duran wine for a change. It was certainly much stronger than Sudran wine and the bouquet was earthy.

"We have our own colosseum, although it's nowhere near as popular or impressive as your own," the emperor offered. "Perhaps we should pay it a visit once you're settled."

"I would like that," Nymati said, her honesty in that moment surprising her. Was that really something she would like? Certainly, she would enjoy the battle, but it felt much like setting a date and she had no intentions of becoming attached to the emperor.

"It's actually owned by one of my cousins. I don't doubt he would appreciate your input on ways he could improve things."

"Surely our mere attendance would do much to bolster ticket sales."

"I guess it would. I imagine many would pay good money for the chance to glimpse the legendary Demon Queen of Sudra."

"You flatter." She blushed, holding his violet gaze before promptly returning to her wine.

In a moment of weakness and honest introspection with herself, Nymati warmed to her position, the allure of becoming empress offering all manner of temptation. On occasion, she caught herself staring at the emperor, forgetting who she was, what he had done, and appreciating all the emperor had become. She continued sipping wine as she admired his strong jaw and taut biceps. Her cheeks warmed and a quiver ran down through her entire body.

He really was quite handsome…

And she was growing hungry…

* * *

Callius chortled, his hand to his chest.

"I have to say, I've never met anyone anywhere near as intimidating as your mother-in-law," Callius admitted, refilling his goblet. "I doubt even a crown would tempt me to marry into her family."

"She was a menace," Nymati sniggered. "It took me far longer than I would have liked to win *that* woman over."

Callius grinned and gulped down wine to fill a lull in the conversation. His evenings with Nymati were becoming the highlight of his trip, but he was still careful to keep up his defences around her. He would have to get over it eventually, but for now, he could not be entirely certain she wasn't planning to kill him. Nor would he blame her for wishing to do so.

Nymati had been an unequalled ally and confidant since the occupation of Sudra, and he had grown to rely on her guidance faster than anticipated. With his father gone, he had no equal for so long it was nice to have someone willing to challenge and even improve on his ideas. Especially when his own queen had proven little use in this aspect.

Sure, Marella attended all the parties and tended the womanly things expected of a queen, proving herself adequate enough. However, she had died in childbirth and the child had been stillborn, leaving Callius heartbroken and without an heir. Sadly, Marella had been mildly inadequate in most aspects of her queendom, at least in retrospect. Nymati, however...

Nymati was intelligent and beautiful, the mother of two strong boys. She was loved by her people and led with grace, but more than that she was strong and practical, maybe even a little ruthless – *and he liked that*. She was everything he had ever wanted in a queen and more, he could think of none more suited to becoming his empress.

"You've never been to Dura before, have you?" he asked, topping up his wine. Nymati held her goblet over the table, allowing him to do the same with hers. "I always assumed I missed you at my wedding. I was really intoxicated come evening."

"No, not once," she corrected. "I was pregnant with Malaki and couldn't attend. You did send an invite though."

"You would've liked my wife," he said, pausing to sup another serving of wine. "Marella was very fond of Sudra in general. Her guard was Sudra, a real quiet lass she was."

"Your wife or the Sudra?"

"The Sudra." Callius stifled a hiccup behind his hand. "Couldn't shut Marella up if I tried. Terrible gossip she was. Always whispering to one person or another."

Nymati smiled at him again, her eyes fixing on his with slow batting lashes. If she were Dura, Callius would have taken her behaviour as a sign of interest, but he presumed Nymati's intentions were muddied by her tipsy condition. They were reaching the end of their wine after all, and even his cheeks burned, but it was nice.

There was no tension between them as Nymati lounged over the makeshift couch. Straight raven hair fell from her shoulders and over her cleavage like a black waterfall, pooling around the red ruby of her necklace. The dress she wore was a thin netted material that latticed across her dark skin, woven and embroidered strategically in a way that roused his curiosity. Every so often her eyes would catch the flickering lights like flashes of vibrant red to outshine any ruby. Her slate-coloured skin was unaffected by the ravages of time, except for the smallest imperfection by her ebony lips that cracked whenever she laughed.

Callius doubted he would find anyone quite as spectacular as the woman sitting before him. It was never his intention to take her as his empress, but he could hardly be distressed with the situation. After all, Nymati was a beauty and a legend in her own right. Many men would risk his life for the position. Many men had.

Callius adjusted himself, their proximity too much and too little at the same time.

His body trembled, a quiver resting upon his lips.

Did she feel the same?

* * *

CHAPTER THREE

Tharin was strutting back towards the inn. His eyes shone bright as the light of the Life Tree. His lips stretched over his face, virtually beaming, his cheeks sporting crater-sized dimples.

He had returned home earlier that evening to find his family waiting impatiently. They had been furious at him, yet surprisingly uninterested in the quest he vanished on. Although, he soon realised why, once he saw Dalliah.

Tharin's insides squeezed with excitement, replaying the memory over and over in hopes of preserving it forever. He had been so excited to tell Reyla, but, now he was preparing to do so, anxiety struck.

Would Reyla be as disappointed in him as his parents were?

Coming from a poorer background and joining the military, Reyla was hardly the most traditional Frey, but nor did he consider her liberal either. Tharin knew in the eyes of many, he had broken a serious taboo.

But Reyla was his friend, she would be happy for him, right?

Tharin lost his trail of thought as something moved in his periphery. He stopped and turned his eyes to the source to see nothing. His hand hovering over the hilt of his sword,

Tharin scanned the shadows.

Without realising, he had managed to walk straight past the Pavilion and enter Low Town. Here, lots of smaller dwellings were strewn between trees and well-worn paths. Bungalows grown from few trees with leaf-covered roofs were set in close proximity with the soft light of candles flickering inside.

Tharin shook his head, sure his mind was playing tricks on him, and continued walking. He wasn't too far from the inn now and would have to decide what to tell Reyla before he arrived.

He jolted when he saw it.

A large shadow. Overhead. Fast. Darting between the buildings.

Tharin's heart raced, unsure what to do, when alarm bells rang through the city.

DONG DONG DONG

Tharin gave chase.

* * *

"And Chloris thinks these children of the Manastream are to blame for the sickness?" asked Arafrey, thin eyebrows pinched.

"It's possible."

Reyla recounted every detail of their journey for the princess; their quest, the cloaked figure, the dark crystal, the books they had read, and all the possible theories Chloris had. She elaborated far more than she had to, savouring just being in the same room as her princess once more.

"But then why poison the Manastream? Why break into the shrine?" Arafrey paced the shabby room, her robes sweeping the floor as the skirt trailed behind her. "Do you think they're after this Hand of Miera?"

"Again, it's possible," replied Reyla, uneasy with the jump in logic. "Without knowing their motives, there's every chance they only wanted access to the Manastream. The shrines being there could merely be coincidence."

"You don't believe in coincidence." Arafrey turned her head in accusation.

Reyla pursed her lips, unable to argue.

The pair continued their discussion long after the sun went down. Hidden away from the outside world they continued, oblivious to the commotion as it started in the palace. But then bells rang through the forests.

DONG DONG DONG

Reyla rushed to the window, straining her eyes over the roofs of Low Town. The call to action hit her stomach as a figure appeared in the distance - with another in hot pursuit.

Reyla grabbed for her sword without hesitation. One leg out the window, she turned back to Arafrey.

"Lock the window and close the curtains. Stay quiet," Reyla instructed in a whisper. "Do you still trust me?"

"Always."

"You open that door for no one else. I'll be back," Reyla promised, flashing her trademark smile before leaping out the window.

Reyla rolled as she hit the ground. Adrenaline burst through her limbs as she returned to her feet with catlike precision. Heart pounding in her ears, Reyla raced down the empty paths. It was easier for her on the ground, her legs burning with amazing speed as she gained on the two figures.

Soon upon them, she realised the one trailing behind was Tharin. He caught her eye, smirking at the sight of Reyla in base-layers wielding a sword.

She ignored him and willed her limbs to go faster as Tharin gained on the figure. They were only two roofs apart. Then one. Then, as Tharin's feet touched the roof edge, he lunged at the figure. His arms held wide, he tackled the shadowy figure through the air and off the side of the building.

The pair crashed down to the other side of a pine dwelling with no lights on inside. By the time Reyla rounded the corner, the figure was already scrambling to their feet. Her hand reached for her sword.

The figure appeared to be from Dura, judging by his rounded ears, but unnaturally grey skin stretched over his gaunt frame. Purple eyes spun wildly in their sockets as he wobbled on spindly legs. He wailed incoherently as they approached, clawing at his face with bony fingers.

Reyla swung her sword point to meet his chest, holding it firm. Alarm bells still rang out as she closed in on the ghastly form.

DONG DONG DONG

"Surrender and I'll spare your life," Reyla commanded, her voice deep. "Drop to your knees."

"Must… Get… Back…"

Tharin drew his sword with caution, his eyes fixed on the Duran.

"Must… Get… Back…"

The Duran's voice was stressed, unnatural. He stunk of death, and the whites of his eyes bulged, blood-shot and twitching uncontrollably with the rest of his body.

Tharin circled across from Reyla, pointing his sword towards the Duran's back.

"Drop to your knees and surrender," Reyla tried again, but the Duran wasn't listening.

"Need… Back… Must…."

The Duran laughed maniacally, waving his arms around as he flew at Reyla. She braced herself. The palm of her hand pressed firmly against the flat of her sword, she deflected his flailing form. She pulled away allowing Tharin to run past.

Tharin rammed his shield into the Duran's back, hurtling him into a nearby dwelling. The wooden wall cracked and groaned as the Duran bounced off, falling to the floor.

DONG DONG DONG

Reyla studied the Duran as he spun around to face them. He was weak, but his movements were erratic, making him hard to defend against. Their best bet was to take out his legs and slow him down. The two Frey circled.

Reyla tightened her grip around her sword, aiming for his knees. Likely thinking the same, Tharin widened his stance and stared down the Duran. They readied for his advance.

"Must... Get... Get... Gyarrrr!!!"

Reyla recoiled as the Duran howled in pain, ripping at his chest. He tore off his shirt, screaming so loud as to drown out the constant DONG, DONG, DONG of the emergency bells. The skin on his chest burned bright red as an emblem etched itself into the Duran's skin. Light burst forth from every orifice and the Duran dropped to the floor, his jaw held wide as he howled in agony.

The Duran yowled like a scolded canine, until eventually, he just stopped. The beaming light faded away to nothing, leaving the Duran still on the floor.

Reyla waited for him to get back up, but he didn't move. Her breath held, she crept towards the still steaming Duran.

Tharin reached the Duran first. He used the end of his sword to poke the body a few times before rolling it on to its back.

Reyla's nose wrinkled. The Duran's chest still glowed where the light appeared, an acidic vapour seeping from the burns it left behind. It was in the shape of a triangle with a cross in the middle and a single dot around each side, similar to the symbols she remembered from history lessons.

They were still examining the body when the knights of the King's Guard arrived. Captain Valren inspected the body while they gave him their report, his shining armour sporting the white cape of the King's Guard.

"Well done, you two," he offered, clearly distracted. "Wait here. I still have a few questions."

They didn't argue and watched quietly as he barked orders for his men to collect the body, unsure what had transpired.

A sense of dread prickled Reyla's senses. She thought it strange that the King's Guard had been called to capture a thief. The entire might of the Palace Guard descending on a lone Duran seemed excessive. Something was wrong. Very wrong.

Reyla's thoughts returned to Princess Arafrey in a panic. Suddenly eager to return to the inn, she approached Captain Valren to explain the situation, but paused as she overheard Gurrien reporting in.

"And you're sure she's dead?" asked Captain Valren, his long face creased in sorrow. "The princess is missing too. We should start a search party…"

Reyla's heart stopped.

Had she heard that right? Was it true?

If she could, she would have told them at that moment she knew where the princess was. However, when she opened her mouth, nothing came out.

It wasn't possible. It wasn't true.

She tried again but her chest grew tight. Her lips quivered, her body paralysed by unbridled emotions. Her breath caught on invisible hands that coiled around her body and dragged her into the ground.

She couldn't be…

Captain Valren was in full swing of organising his men, his grey ponytail swishing furiously over his white cape as he whipped his head about, when Reyla finally found her voice.

"Sir, I- I know where the princess is."

"You do?" he asked, his stony eyes predatory as he caught her in his sights.

"Yeah, well I know where I left her," Reyla admitted, knowing Valren to be an allegiant Frey.

"Oh?"

"We're on special assignment and were reporting in." That much was true, but it was best to keep the specifics to themselves.

"Right, good job. Secure the princess and return to the palace in the morning, better safe than sorry. Understood?"

The two Frey saluted and went to leave, but Reyla turned back.

She started a few times before finally managing:

"Sir… What do I tell the princess…?"

* * *

CHAPTER FOUR

Midnight came and went.

The guards changed and the servers retired for the evening leaving Nymati alone with the emperor – or at least undisturbed, as there would always be men on patrol.

"So, what made you decide to take Puwhar?" she asked.

"You'll think me hopeless," he said, looking away with embarrassment.

"I promise, I won't," she assured him, her hand to her ruby necklace.

"I had a dream."

"A dream?"

"I assume it was a dream," he replied, his brows knitted. "I was in my bed one night when an angel appeared before me. A creature white as snow with silver eyes and hair. In a voice that haunts me even to this day, they drew me from the depths of my despair and said the time was coming for me to prove myself to the whole planet. They said Alamantra needed to be united to face what was to come. That I was the only one to do it… And… Well, here we are."

He held his hands up as he gestured to the tent.

"Silver hair and eyes?" Nymati repeated, unsure what else she could say.

"See, I told you, you'd think it was stupid."

"No, not at all," she protested, returning her goblet to the table with an uneven hand; she may have indulged a little too much. "I just never expected you to come out with something so *divine*. You really are full of surprises."

Nymati ran a single fang over her bottom lip. She had been holding herself back against the carnal stirrings calling her to action for a while. With their wine long gone, her cigarettes too, the tension in the air was palpable and the hunger within her grew with each passing moment.

She needed to leave, to get as far away from the emperor as possible before she did something she could not take back, but her body had stopped listening to her brain hours before.

"Puwhar was child's play," Callius boasted, his chest puffing with pride. "Once we fully invaded, it didn't take long to mount an assault on Estra. Mighty warriors they are indeed, but so disorganised it didn't take much to confuse and divide them."

Once Callius began telling her of his victories and battles over recent years, all hopes were lost. Nymati became too engrossed in conversation to fight her urges any longer. He was showing off, but she found it endearing. Her tail swirled in figures of eight beside her.

"Did you see much action yourself?" Nymati purred;

the talk of battle never ceased to send her heart racing.

"I couldn't lead the vanguard, but I always made sure to drive the rear in faster than needed so I could join in myself."

It was as if every word that came out of his mouth was designed for her. She ate up every syllable escaping his comely lips.

"Some Estra punk actually managed to catch me with his spear." Callius pulled his toga to show her the scar. "My own fault though. Won't be making that mistake again!"

Nymati chuckled and her eyes fixed on the scar, saliva catching at the corner of her mouth as hunger surged. She chewed the side of her tongue, and tried to suppress her growing appetite, but it was all she could think about.

She'd never tasted a Duran before. She wondered what they tasted like. She wondered what the emperor would taste like. Not that she could or would, of course. She was strong enough to withhold herself.

Nymati pushed into the crate furniture as if to restrain herself, her stomach rumbling.

The emperor looked like he would taste real nice.

It had been so long since she had fed too… They were getting married, it was hardly taboo… And she was hungry.

So very, very, hungry…

* * *

It was very early morning.

Callius had long since run out of things to talk about, as had Nymati, and they fell into that intoxicated lull which so very often happens after several refills of wine and a long day. It was nice, he could not remember a time he ever felt so comfortable just sitting with another person, which was weird considering who that person was.

He rubbed his jaw, the stubble fast reappearing as their night continued.

Who was Nymati anyway? Although they had met many years ago, he hardly knew her, yet somehow he felt they were close.

"Could I ask you a question?" he started, clearing his throat as if to sober himself. "The story of the Septirrian Thief. I've always wondered how you would be able to chase down a thief only to be caught by a bunch of bandits."

"That's because you are mixing two tales," Nymati told him, waving two fingers in his general direction. "There was one thief who stole the Septirrian, but I stopped him."

"You did?"

"I did," she agreed, her intonation rising. "The bastard managed to make it out of the palace too. Can't have that, can we? So, I flew out and got him."

"You make it sound so easy."

"That's because it was. They don't call me the Demon Queen for nothing, you know." She winked.

Callius nearly swallowed his tongue. Was she flirting

with him? No, she couldn't possibly be.

The emperor blushed, although his cheeks were already flushed from the wine, so there was hope Nymati wouldn't notice. "So, what was the other one?"

Nymati squinted, having already forgotten what they were talking about.

"You said it was two stories. So then, what was the other one?"

"Oh right. Yes," she slurred, pouting as she arranged her thoughts. "The ambushing. Mere coincidence, the bandits hit the wrong cart. They killed my men. I got mad. People lost their heads. You know how it is."

He chuckled, awestruck.

Nymati was so calm, so cool, so completely and utterly indifferent. So cruel and ferocious, and yet a beacon of love and hope across Sudra. It was all rather strange to the Duran emperor, but he was starting to understand it.

Sure, he was still wary of her, every fibre of his being told him he should be, yet she had been nothing but perfection since the moment they were reunited. There was a brief moment he worried the loss of Drazah may have been too much for Nymati, but she soon recovered, especially after he proposed marriage.

"I wonder what they will call you now," he mused aloud, a flutter of excitement through his stomach as he considered the possibilities. Demon Empress perhaps. "You were just a princess when I first met you, was it the thief that earned you your title?"

"Now, that is a story for another time," she teased.

Callius grinned. Although their first encounter had been brief, he remembered it as if it were yesterday. He had taken Nymati by the hand and kissed it as his family wished the newly-weds good luck at their wedding. Her fingers had been so soft. Warm and comforting. His fingers had brushed over her many golden rings, his heart skipping more and more as he pulled her hand to meet his teenage lips.

Were her hands still so soft? His eyes followed her movement, but he couldn't see for the gloves she wore. Gloves she wore for a very good reason.

The emperor swallowed the notion with what remained of his wine. It would be a lie to say he wasn't tempted. In fact, it was quite the opposite. Sweat traced his hairline. It was becoming too much for him to hide. His pulse throbbed in his extremities, in other places too. His mouth ran dry, catching his words.

He yearned to feel her touch on his skin, damn the consequences. He needed to know what it would feel like to take her in his arms, kiss her ebony lips and run his hands through her hair. She had yet to touch him, and yet she pulled him in with her ruby eyes.

His heart pounded. There were too many reasons for him to ignore the overwhelming need that filled him - but they quickly vanished as their eyes met. Was it possible that she felt it too?

There was only really one way for him to find out.

Screw it.

* * *

Alone outside, an observer smiled through a crack in the tent as the emperor descended on Nymati.

She stepped back and congratulated herself on a job well done. It was like watching two puppets dance.

Although her sisters would not approve, she no longer felt Mother was up to the challenge of leading them or dealing with the Empire. She had no choice but to take matters into her own hands. Mother had gone soft; *she* needed to manage the situation.

They couldn't just sit back and wait.

She was surprised the Noctinka had worked so well, and again commended herself on the job she had done.

She was clearly the most talented of her sisters at so many things. Should anything happen to Mother, she would be the perfect, if not only, candidate to take her place.

A loud rip and a flutter tore from the tent as Nymati spread her wings, her silhouette painted in candlelight against the tent wall. She wrapped around the emperor, her artes flowing freely as she sunk her fangs into his neck. Wood shattered as the emperor roared. He threw Nymati into the furniture and lunged after her.

The observer smirked at the amusing turn of events. Who would have thought Nymati and Callius held sparks for one another? No matter. The pair would still rip each other to shreds by the morning. Once both Nymati and the emperor were dead, she would call out Mother's failings, then take her place as head of the Sisterhood.

Yes, she could see it now…

* * *

CHAPTER FIVE

Reyla slouched uncomfortably over the bed in the inn.

It was difficult, but Reyla was the one who told the princess of Elsafrey's demise. Arafrey cried hysterically, clinging to Reyla like a safety blanket, until eventually crying herself to sleep.

Reyla still held Arafrey tight, her tunic damp with tears as she cradled the sleeping princess in her arms. The thin pillows sank behind her, disappearing into the mattress, offering little support. Her neck leant awkwardly over the headboard, pressing her head against the wall. Reyla's thumb stroked across Arafrey's soft skin habitually, her hazel eyes surveying their surroundings with a burning intensity.

"You should get some sleep," Reyla whispered. Tharin perched on the bed opposite, his face aghast. "I got this."

"You sure?"

Reyla gave a gentle nod, letting him know it was okay. Tharin then collapsed fully dressed to the bed without argument, leaving Reyla's eyes to return to the door. She watched as candle light flickered against the wooden wall. Devoid of emotions, she followed the shadows dancing over the rotten furnishings.

A pang of guilt rolled through her stomach at her ease in holding the princess close once more. She was practically elated to have Arafrey in her arms. Granted her shirt was soggy and Tharin snored in the bed across from them, but it was nice. Although, it wasn't going to help her move on any time soon.

Her parents, her comrades and now her queen. She had seen so much death in her time, perhaps she had just grown numb to it. Although, she had taken a fair share of lives herself, so it was probably best she didn't think about it too seriously.

Reyla drew a deep breath, lavender perfume taking her back to nights not long ago she would hold her dear princess like this, praying things would never have to change.

But alas, this was only the start of things to come…

* * *

CHAPTER SIX

No one dared enter the emperor's tent the next morning.

The two guards on duty, Privates Gage and Rentin, spent most of their shift blushing or shifting awkwardly as they pretended not to listen to the amorous activities behind them. It was a team decision that they would allow the emperor to sleep through his morning wake up call. Should anyone ask, they all agreed to forget whose job it was to wake him that morning.

They remained at their posts, held to attention in anticipation of their orders, but were torn away when they heard a high-pitched scream...

* * *

Emperor Gabris had stirred awake mere moments earlier.

He stretched out, aware of the uneven, strangely solid surface beneath him, his eyelids still too heavy to raise. His body hummed with ecstasy. In all his life he could not remember ever feeling so relaxed and comfortable. It was as if each of his muscles had received their own massage for several hours before being left in a warm soak for a day or two.

Then it came.

His senses were assaulted by the unnatural shriek. He jolted upright, black spots across his vision as his eyes adjusted to Nymati standing blood-soaked and naked before him.

Callius recoiled, preparing to defend himself as Nymati posed ready to attack, her eyes darting around with confused fury. He blinked in quick succession as if to wake himself from a dream. Try as he might, Callius remembered little from the previous night and was also wildly confused. He looked down frowning, finding himself in a similar state of bloody undress.

Where did the blood come from? Why were they naked? Why were they on the floor?

His attention returned to Nymati as black leathery wings tore from her back, wrapping around her womanly frame. She snarled, an arm reaching from her cocoon as she snatched a cloth from the floor before storming for the exit.

Callius remained dazed and confused, staring at the dust cloud Nymati left behind her.

He had never seen her wings before. They were much smaller than Drazah's. He had never had the cause to ask about a woman's transformation - and he wondered how else they differed.

Callius shook his head clear and gathered himself,

sighing at the sight of his dishevelled tent.

The crates used to make their furniture had seen most of the damage, many of them had been splintered beyond repair and strewn across the floor. Pillows had burst, throws were torn, and their clothes had been shredded. Most worrisome of all, everything was splattered with blood. Not just splattered, the sandy floor clumped where pools soaked into the ground and lines of arterial spray ran across the fabric walls of the tent.

Callius cursed to himself as he found his toga. It was torn down the front and still dripped with blood. His eyebrows pressed as he tried to clear his mind, but whenever he tried to remember what had happened his head only hurt more. He couldn't believe he had blacked out. He was usually so good at holding his liquor and of all the nights to decide to over-do it he chose *last* night.

No matter how hard he tried, the last thing he remembered was... He was sitting, talking with Nymati... And then... No, there was nothing.

Did they drink that much?

He didn't remember drinking that much.

Frustration bubbled in the pit of his stomach. Something was going on. He wasn't sure what, but whatever it was, it ruined all the work he had put in with Nymati and he was furious. However, the sight of her standing over him lingered in his thoughts - making it hard to stay mad.

He smirked. *I guess she doesn't hate me after all.*

Callius grabbed a fresh set of clothes from his trunk,

admiring his body while he dressed.

He felt amazing. Every part of his body was energized. Aches and pains he had lived with for years were gone and some of his lesser scars had vanished. Which begged the question, where was the blood from? Did it come from them?

Callius returned to the mess of crates, his eye catching on Nymati's ruby necklace lying among the wreckage. He collected it with delicate hands, unable to remember a time he had seen Nymati without it. He hoped she was okay.

Alongside the necklace, he found one of their goblets from the previous evening. The inside of the golden surface was now stained, but not the colour of wine, it was almost green. He sniffed at the goblet, recoiling as a foul smell ravaged his senses and threatened the lining of his stomach.

Callius cast the goblet aside and marched from his tent. He turned to the two unsuspecting guards posted by the door, fire burning behind his violet eyes.

"Has anyone passed by you?" he barked.

The two guards turned to each other with uncertainty. Their faces paled as they scrambled to answer, each glancing to Nymati's tent before looking at him.

"Aside from Nymati," Callius confirmed, reducing his temper somewhat.

"No, Sir, not since we came on duty last night," said one, with a salute.

Callius expected this, no staff were to enter his tent without a reason after the last guard change.

"Who was on duty before you?" he asked, not waiting for a response. "I want you to bring them to me immediately."

"Yes, Sir," they replied before running away.

Callius turned to see a concerned Commander Raltz.

"Tell the men we're staying put another night," Callius ordered. "I want the patrols doubled, and I want the names of everyone who served us last night."

"Yes, sire," Raltz replied with a humble bow. "Anything else?"

"Yes! Send Hellard to tidy my tent!"

* * *

CHAPTER SEVEN

Reyla could still smell Arafrey's lavender fragrance on her clothes as they arrived in the palace the next morning. She skulked through the quiet corridors to the throne hall.

Two guards stood to attention on either side of the door to the king's office, each sporting the steel armour and white capes of the King's Guard. They each held still as muffled shouting penetrated the thick oak.

"Are you sure you're up to this?" asked Reyla, pulling Arafrey aside.

"Yes. He needs to know the full story or else–"

"Or else it could start a war with the Empire," Reyla finished. "If you want, we can–"

"No. No. You need to get going," Arafrey insisted. "The sun will be up soon."

They held each other's gaze, each silently wishing they could voice their heartfelt goodbyes.

Was this goodbye?

Reyla studied every inch of her princess; her hair unbrushed and scruffy, her eyes red and puffy, her cheeks raw. There was no one in Alamantra she cared for more, and her heart broke at the prospect of leaving her princess at the time when she needed her most.

"Our kingdom needs you now more than ever," Reyla warned, swallowing as her eyes stung.

"Promise me," she forced out. The words were like coals on her tongue, her heart trembling as she built the courage to speak the words she had always hoped would never pass her lips. "We have to move forward. It's…

"It's time we grow up…"

Arafrey stepped back as she righted herself, nodding her head through tear filled eyes. Sucking air through her nose, she gathered her strength and replied:

"I promise."

* * *

For the second time in as many months, Reyla left her princess alone and in tears. She remained sullen, her heart broken all over again, as she and Tharin left the palace and headed for the depot.

The skies were dark and dismal. It was as if the whole forest was mourning with them as they trudged through the depressed training grounds. A light rain caused a thin mist to fall over the forest, as animals lay still and the plants stood weeping.

Soldiers hung their heads low in sorrow as they returned red-eyed and pale-faced to the barracks after an endless night, too shaken to speak. Horses in the paddocks lay down in the spray, making no attempts to greet them as they normally would. Even the endlessly energetic retriever the men had adopted, chose to lay in a puddle in the middle of the sparring pit.

Expecting it to be empty, Tharin pushed open the wooden door to the depot rakishly, surprising the Frey on the other side as the door bounced off the frame. The depot was usually run by Map Flinley, an old Frey who had been there almost as long as the palace itself, but it was Mika who stood behind the long wooden counter that morning.

They greeted Mika warmly, or as well as they could manage, having served beside him many times over the years.

"Shut the door," he called, his voice a deep baritone that twanged with a northern accent. "Was told you'd be coming but after… Well, just glad to see you're alright. It's not been the same without you."

The two Frey gave Mika wry smiles as they tried to push past the loss haunting them. He still wore his Queen's Guard uniform, and his seaweed coloured hair was tied back into a long single braid highlighting the silver bands around his ears. His fox-red eyes rested upon the heavy black bags of someone who had not slept in far too long.

Mika didn't wait for a response. He lifted up two large packs and bedrolls on to the counter.

"Elsafrey – rest her spirit – her last orders were for me to pack and equip you." Mika grinned as the two handed over their packs. "She even gave old man Flinley the day off, so I could raid all the good stuff he hides in back."

He pulled out two new swords and shields - each lacking the notches and worn handles of their former gear. Mika also laid out new travelling cloaks and leaf-leather armours, their current duds already soot laden and stale.

"She also gave me this," he added, throwing a sizeable bag of coins to Reyla. "I know it's all hush hush, but whatever it is you're doing, just come back in one piece."

"We'll be back before you know it." Tharin smirked, heaving his pack on to his shoulders. Reyla gave a nod in agreement, still not quite ready to speak. "We should have some tales to tell once we're done too."

"Then the first round shall be on me," declared Mika as he clapped his hand against Tharin's pack. He followed them from the depot into the dismal training ground. "Good luck, my friends. And may the Gods be with you."

"And you," Reyla finally managed, her heart heavy as she took in the palace one last time.

* * *

CHAPTER EIGHT

The kingdom of Freya was on high alert and wracked with sorrow. The skies were bleak and the citizens gloomy as our dear princess stood alone in the throne hall, watching through tear-filled eyes as her beloved walked away from her for the second time in as many months.

Her heart heavy and her body drained, Arafrey entered her father's office unnoticed, to find him red-faced and raging.

"I will not stand for this," he bellowed, the vein on his neck bulging as he spat at a stone-faced Captain Valren. "How did a Duran even make it through the forests unnoticed to begin with? What is the point of having a patrol unit if they let anyone pass?"

"He may have used magic to get past them, Sire. The blade used was coated in some unknown toxin which prevents artes from healing the wound. The two guards who took him down also said he appeared to be bewitched," Captain Valren offered. "Before he died, a rune etched itself into the man's chest, and he was desperately incoherent."

Arafrey sighed. The mysterious blade corroborated Reyla's theory, but still begged the question of why. Why did the witches kill her mother?

"Are we to believe the Empire is using magic now?" spat Galafrey, still oblivious to her entry.

"You think if they could bewitch people, they would send one of their men?" snapped Arafrey without thinking. "Why not one from Sheya or Pudron?"

Galafrey stopped, finally realising she was there. Stone returned to his face, her resemblance to Elsafrey forcing a quiet to wash over him. He rounded the desk to take Arafrey in his arms, holding her tightly.

"You should go get some sleep, dear." He sighed as he brushed tangled hair behind Arafrey's pointed ears.

"I'm fine," Arafrey insisted, waving him off. "Besides I have much to tell you."

The Frey king smiled weakly in agreement and returned to his chair. His face once again expressionless, he turned his attention back to Captain Valren.

"Were there any other casualties?"

"I'm afraid so," Valren replied. "It seems two guards at the temple were killed, another injured, and the priestess' office ransacked."

"Any witnesses?" asked Galafrey, his voice back to its normal monotone.

"The injured guard had little to say, but one of the patients, Nasir of the Princess' Guard, saw a woman exiting the office before heading to the catacombs."

"A woman?"

"Well, he thinks it was a woman," Valren reported. "She was rather small and wearing a hooded cloak. He's in one of the wards though and only heard through the door as she took down the guards, so he can't be certain."

Arafrey's heart sank. Was her mother's death merely a distraction? Who would do such a thing?

"So, our Duran was not alone," mused Galafrey. "Inform all the men, I want the guards doubled. There will be no days off for the time being. I want two men at every post, even in the evenings, and if anyone passes into my borders, I want to be the first one to hear about it. Understood?"

"Understood."

Captain Valren hurried away, leaving Arafrey alone with her father.

"I received a report from Reyla last night before everything went down," she stated, studying her father's lack of reaction. "She and Tharin just set off for Sheya."

"Who?"

"The guards who helped take down the Duran," Arafrey replied, her eyes narrowing as they threatened to roll.

She was never able to decide if it was arrogance or poor memory which caused her father to be so incapable of remembering names. Either way, it had always caused her much frustration.

"The two sent to find the cure for the sickness."

"Ah yes, yes, now I remember…"

"When were you planning on telling me witches were poisoning the Manastream? That there's no cure to the sickness?" she accused, adopting her father's signature tone of unbridled disappointment and quiet fury. Having been on the receiving end of it many times, she was becoming quite proficient.

"When it became pertinent that you knew."

Arafrey could feel her sorrow being quickly replaced by fury, but held her tongue. She summarised what Reyla told her about the spirit in Pudron and the theories they had, but neglected to mention Chloris.

"Reyla and Tharin have reason to suspect the same witches are to blame for the Duran. It's possible they were the ones who ransacked the temple."

"It could just be a coincidence but it's best we double the patrol to be sure," Galafrey agreed, much to her surprise. "However, I think, for now, you should go get some sleep." He looked to her with glossy eyes, his high cheekbones holding heavy black bags, and sat back quietly in his chair. "There will be time for work and mourning once you are rested."

Arafrey gave a weak nod in response, quietly making her exit.

She crossed the throne hall, the sound of two pairs of guard's feet following close behind her as she ascended the wooden stairs to her bedroom. Her bottom lip trembled as she walked, her facade holding a turbulent storm of emotions in place.

Arafrey closed the bedroom door behind her before dropping to the floor.

She curled into herself, sobbing into her hands in hopes of muffling the sound from the guards outside. Tears finally escaped her emerald eyes, her chest heaving as she cursed the cruel, twisted fate that would take both her mother and Reyla away from her in the same night.

Exhausted, she closed her eyes, the wooden floor cool against her burning cheeks. And there she remained, alone with her pain, for the rest of the day.

* * *

CHAPTER NINE

Tharin was a mix of emotions as they left the training grounds, following the city streets north, until they reached the boundary of the Life Tree's glow. They stopped once more and looked along the Freya road leading to the Sheya border together.

Their usual routine feeling rather disrespectful, they chose only to stand still. Their eyes closed, their heads bowed, they bid farewell to the queen and high priestess they loved so much. Each prayed she found peace.

Reyla began walking when Tharin looked back over his shoulder. "You think everyone will be okay?"

"They will be once we get the Hand." Reyla turned back to flash a reassuring smile.

Tharin paused, allowing her words to sink in. His depression shrank, suddenly replaced with burning ambition and restless energy that filled his body.

For the first time in his life, Tharin had a task set before him so great that he was excited and scared, but also exhilarated and sad. It was so strange. Each emotion bounced around his insides like pins and needles.

It was a feeling unlike any other. He had drive. A

purpose. For Dalliah, Elsafrey, and all those plagued with the sickness, he couldn't fail. He must keep going.

Was this how soldiers felt as they marched into battle?

Did this make him a real soldier?

Tharin cast one last glance over the forest city, his heart swelling.

"Don't worry," Reyla added. "Only eight more blessings to go."

"*Only,*" Tharin mocked, rolling his eyes as he ran to catch up with her.

* * *

CHAPTER TEN

It took the better part of the morning to clean up the mess in his tent, giving Callius time to interrogate the two guards. His line of questioning was soon proven pointless as they were only able to name the Duran staff. Although the names they gave did match the list Raltz had collected, which was a small positive.

He drew a deep breath of crisp air, still uncomfortable in the warm autumn climate, his eyes on Nymati's tent. There had been no noise or movement from within all day. His fingers tightened around the ruby of her necklace as he fought the urge to return it to her.

Callius entered his tent, unsettled.

As his headache faded, he managed to piece together bits of the previous night. Snippets of conversation and flashes of memory trickled into clarity, although not enough to help place the blame on any one person.

Callius hunkered down on a cushion and reread the list of staff from Raltz. There were three members of Nymati's staff to interview, but he felt it best to speak with her before doing so. He was ashamed to admit that, while he recognised the names on the lists, he couldn't place them, nor did he remember them serving him last night - or any other for that matter.

Callius followed the bloodstains along the tent wall as he pondered.

Of course, knowing the delivery system was only part of the puzzle. It would be difficult to deduce what the poison was while in the field. Was it even poison they were given? He was finding it hard to think of any poison that would cause whatever had happened last night.

An outsider would be quick to blame Nymati, but he had quickly decided that was not the case. Her reaction and the fact she left her necklace behind were all the proof he needed of her innocence.

"Excuse me, Sire."

Callius started as Raltz entered his tent holding dinner plates. Without realising, he had spent all afternoon deep in thought.

"I brought your dinner," Raltz offered, placing the plate on the newly built table. "I watched them make it myself, just to be sure."

"Thanks." The job was beneath his Commander, but it was best to keep news of the attempt on his life to as few people as possible. "Assign someone you trust next time."

"Shall do. And what should I do with Lady Nymati's supper?"

"Leave it here, best let her be," Callius replied, hopeful food would be enough to draw her from her tent. "Let one of her staff know it's here."

"Would you like me to fetch wine whilst I'm at it?"

Callius hesitated. "Please."

He made no attempts to begin eating, instead choosing to wait and see if Nymati came to join him.

To his disappointment, Raltz was the next person to enter his tent, a fresh bottle of wine in hand. He uncorked the bottle and sniffed the contents before placing it beside his dinner plate.

"Anything else, Sir?"

"No, you're dismissed."

"As you wish," replied Raltz with a bow.

Raltz returned to the door, halting as Nymati entered. He quickly moved out of her way and bowed his head to let her pass.

Callius' whole body lit up forcing him to his feet, his heart skipping.

"I didn't think you were coming," he breathed once the door fell closed.

Nymati indicated the table with two plates of food.

"I had hope." He smiled.

"I'm sorry I'm late." She bowed her head and took her seat across from him.

The pair fell back into their awkward silence. It had been so long, he had almost forgotten how uncomfortable it made him. He just had to start talking. It was that easy, in theory. But how to bring up a subject so complicated without causing it to become more awkward?

Callius cleared his throat. "About last night–"

"Did I hurt you?" Her brow wrinkled with her concern.

"No. No, I'm fine, amazing in fact."

"That's good…"

Nymati smiled softly, causing him to smile back. He didn't like seeing Nymati so vulnerable, but it was rather charming to see her softer side.

"I want you to know I've increased security just to be sure. And all food and wine will be made under the strictest supervision."

Nymati paused, her whole demeanour changing.

"You don't think it was me?" She sighed through her nose as the tension appeared to drop from her shoulders. "Thank you…"

"Well, you seemed pretty surprised this morning, so…"

They laughed together.

"Oh. And you left something behind." Callius presented her necklace with a valorous smile.

Nymati grasped at her neck in panic as if suddenly realising it were missing. Her gloveless fingers brushed over his hardened palm as she snatched it back to the safety of her bosom.

"The clasp is broken, but we can get it fixed once we get back home," he offered, hoping the gesture was enough to repair some of the damage done.

"This necklace is very precious to me," she breathed, clutching the necklace to her chest. "Thank you."

The tent fell quiet, the tension significantly reduced, but not quite what it was before.

"I'll find who did this," he promised her, fire burning through his body like cheap brandy. Callius reached to place his hand over hers. "I'll make them pay for this."

That night, in a tent, in an unnamed patch of sand, a bond was formed. A raging inferno joined the emperor with a demon and, in the blink of an eye, the strongest two beings in the whole of Alamantra became comrades.

"No..." Nymati hissed, her eyes narrow.

"We'll make them pay."

* * *

CHAPTER ELEVEN

While citizens slept, three sisters gathered.

"Ah, Ren," came a soft voice from under a dark cloak. "Where's Mother?"

"She's busy," she replied bluntly, under orders to say no more. They ducked further into the shadows as a third cloaked figure came to join them. "How did things go in Freya?"

"Not great, the two Frey have certainly taken the blessings," replied the soft-spoken one. "I followed them halfway to Sheya before turning back."

"And Elsafrey?"

"Dead."

"Good." That was a small positive, at least their plan hadn't been a complete failure. Still, their Mother was unlikely to be pleased when she discovered they missed out on the Ancestor's blessings, and she considered having one of her sisters deliver the news for her.

"You think Freya will attack the Empire?" asked the brazen one.

"With any luck, but for now our orders are to return to

base and stay put," she replied, to much protest.

"What about the blessings?" asked one.

"What's Mother thinking?" asked the other.

"Look I'm not happy about it either, but orders are orders," she explained, holding her hands up before them. "There's nothing we can do about it."

Neither seemed satisfied with her answer, but they decided not to argue - after all, Mother's word was law.

"What about the Empire?" huffed the brazen one.

"Mother's dealing with it," she replied, although she believed it as much as they did. "Look, we need to keep the Empire distracted or our whole plan is at stake. She wouldn't let us down. Not with something so important."

"I dunno, Ren… It's just not the same," said the soft-spoken one, toying with the cuffs of her sleeve. "She seems…"

"Weak," the other finished, her tone bitter. "She's scared, sad and pathetic. She should be ordering us to kill people ourselves not have some Duran do the dirty work. He almost got caught too!"

"She has a point. You were right to have us mark him."

She didn't argue, but she didn't defend her Mother either. With her potion failing, she had to find new ways to undermine their absent leader if she wished to take Mother's place. Fortunately, her sisters were not the wisest of creatures.

"Just be patient, I'm sure Mother has a plan," she

promised. "For now, we should do as we're told and return to base."

Her sisters voiced their anger before leaving, their grievances only solidifying her resolve.

It was just a matter of time…

* * *

THE LIGHT OF MIERA BOOK ONE:

A Guard's Refrain

To Be Continued...

ACKNOWLEDGMENTS

Thank you everyone who made it this far.

Releasing A Guard's Request in two parts to create A Guard's Refrain was not a decision I took lightly, but with A Prelude to Light under my belt and readers hungry for more, it felt like the correct decision for me and my community. Thank you all for your support, I couldn't do any of this without you.

I was just a person with an idea and no way to get it out, until Craig Hallam told me to plan a D&D campaign. That plan became the bones of this story and it's thanks to him that I'm the author I am today. It's a pleasure to know such an amazing author, but equally you can all blame him for the months and years I've spent ignoring my friends to continue writing. Thanks Craig!

Amy Wilson came in and saved the day for this series in general. My incredible writing friend and editor, this book would not have gone to print without her hard work, support and selflessness. She is a talented author I'm honoured to work alongside.

ArtWomble also came in at the last minute to replace my cover art and help bring my vision to life. He is an artist who always inspires me and those around him - you should definitely check out his Twitch!

There are so many people who helped me through the early stages of writing, without whom I would never have passed the first draft. Mulukh, thank you for helping me develop my style and talking me down whenever I got overwhelmed by the standards I set myself. My endless gratitude and love goes to Schwifty for listening as I worked through story points and giving me wrestling tips for battle scenes. And Geej, for being my writing buddy since high school and for introducing me to Sanderson's lectures on YouTube, where I found Jenna Moreci and her incredible tutorials.

Brook Rogers and R T Strange, my Shark Tank survivors and comrades in arms. It's been a heckin' long journey, but you've been my support and guides throughout it all. From enthusiastic minotaurs to emotional goodbyes, I'm super proud of how far we've all come.

Many thanks to my beta readers and Book Club viewers on Twitch. I kept hurting you and you kept coming back for more, which is more than any author could wish for. Your love for my characters and endless encouragement are what kept me going through this whole process. And it was a long process.

And finally, Papa Mash, my biggest fan and supporter. I've come a long way in recent years, and none of that would be possible without him. Most parents would rather their kids held more sensible ambitions, but my Dad was always proud of me no matter what I do. I miss him every day.

This book is dedicated to Nelly. I know she would be so proud of all of us and all we've accomplished. She was a mother to many, and we all miss her greatly.

Thanks for reading!

Ash

ABOUT THE AUTHOR

Ash Hester started her career in comics and animation, but always had a love for storytelling and fantasy. Contributing to several indie press projects, she later founded Niche: Treat Your Geek to showcase news and reviews featuring the many talented people within her reach. Fuelled by Anime, Television and Video Games, her imagination shows no bounds, leading her to begin writing her first epic fantasy novel in 2019. Venturing deeper into the nerd havens of Twitch and Twitter, she found herself welcomed within the D&D and TTRPG community and featured in several Actual Plays.

Yorkshire born and Scottish grown, Ash always gravitated towards geeky circles. Raised on a healthy diet of Star Trek and Pokemon, she found herself on the anime, cosplay and sci-fi convention circuits in her university years. With many years in and around the industry, she continued to encourage the passions of others and inspired others with her writing advice on her Twitch and TikTok.

If you have enjoyed this book, please consider leaving a review for Ash Hester on Amazon or Goodreads to let her know what you thought of her work.

Website: www.authorahester.uk